Thrown into Love Copy

Gigi Hodge

Contents

Dedication

To my husband, for everything you do and especially for your two-day trek through mountains, lakes, and jungles to get my new computer!

1

Tangled Web

Renee

I glared up at Principal James. I was used to looking down on his bald spot when I spoke with him. Instead, I was flat on my back on the floor. I scanned my surroundings. I was in my classroom. Still colorful, still messy, but devoid of students.

"What happened?" I asked.

"Isn't it obvious? You fainted." Principal James frowned down at me, his hands on his hips. I glared at him, knowing that my ice-blue eyes made him fidgety. "Don't glare at me. You know the issue," he growled.

"I do?" Lifting myself onto my elbows, I pulled out my bun, and finger combed my locks. God knows what playground *gradoue* my students tracked in on the bottom of their shoes. My ash blonde hair, always a magnet for dirt, showed every bit of grime and dust.

He stared at my stomach and then glared back at me. "Don't play dumb, *Miss* Babineaux"

"Excuse me? I don't know what you're talking about." I mean, I could guess, but I wasn't certain. With a huff, I pulled my phone out of my pocket, turned it on, and called the office.

"You're not supposed to have your phone on at school." Jamesy did not move; he continued to glower down at me.

I rolled my eyes and hit the speakerphone. "It wasn't on. I just turned it on. You saw me turn it on."

"Why? You need to put that away." He reached for the phone, and I turned to my side, hiding the phone under my boob. Let's see you try to grab it now. He was griping about something, but I ignored his blather and spoke to the secretary. "Mrs. Broussard? This is Renee Babineaux in room twelve."

"Yes, Renee dear? What can I do for you?"

"Mrs. Broussard. You're on speaker phone. Did Mr. James have you call for an ambulance?"

"Heavens no. Why would he?"

"Well, apparently, I fainted. And rather than make sure that there wasn't something wrong with me and get me the medical help I needed, he decided to come down here and watch me as I was passed out on the floor and then glare at me when I woke up. Can you call for medical help and get me a work injury form? I will need to fill that out to make sure the school pays for the ambulance and my medical care."

"Why that no good, *fils d'putain* [son of a bitch]! Of course, dear. You stay on the floor. I will have someone take care of your class for the rest of the day."

"Thanks Ms. B," I said, then hung up the phone.

"There is no reason for an ambulance," Jamesy grunted as he leaned down to reach for me in an effort to haul me up.

"Touch me and I scream," I told him. "You're the one that decided that a teacher passed out on the ground was not worth fretting over. Now you can fret about your budget and explain to the board why your workers' comp is so high."

"You know, if you go through workers' comp, then we get the medical records." He crossed his arms over his chest, the too-small suit straining at his shoulders.

"So?"

Jamesy sneered. "We have a moral turpitude clause in your contract. If you're pregnant and unmarried, we can fire you."

"This is not the 19th century, Jamesy. Whatever. Just get away from me — your cologne is making me nauseous. I promise, if I throw up because of your smell, I *will* aim at your fancy loafers."

He jumped back, muttering about how my test scores weren't worth this hassle. I ignored him as he huffed and left the room. I called my mama and Tante Em right away, knowing that Ms. B's call, right after she called for an ambulance, would be to them. Then I dialed my best friend Kayleigh to pick me up from the hospital.

As I waited for the ambulance, I wondered if Jamesy was right. He was a prick, but he was an observant one. I laid a protective hand on my stomach, grabbed my purse, and hoped.

Once the ambulance delivered me to the hospital, I waited in an emergency room bed. I rifled through my purse as I waited for the doctor with the test results. Out of my wallet, I pulled a folded picture of the Krewe — a Mardi Gras social group, though really just my friends. My gaze scanned every face but kept fixating on the giant at the back. With his black hair, coal-black eyes, and pale skin, Armand could have been cast for the various vampire shows set in Louisiana. When the doctor opened the curtain, I snuck the photo back into my wallet and braced for the verdict. Fingers crossed.

Hah! Jamesy was right! I smiled to myself. I was indeed pregnant. Dr. Woods broke the news to me, but it wasn't all good. She thought I needed to restrict my activity because of my elevated blood pressure. During our interview, my mama and Tante Em barged in because apparently doctor patient privilege did not apply to them.

Which is why Tante Em interrupted our discussion to ask, "What about the two flights of stairs up to her apartment, Dr. Woods? Can Renee climb them while she's on restricted activity?"

Dr. Woods shook her head. "Absolutely not. Verboten. Not only because of the strain, but also because she already fainted once — you wouldn't want her to fall down the stairs."

My mama was having trouble hiding her glee. "Then you will have to move back home."

"I'm not moving back home, Mama. I'm a grown woman."

She turned to Tante Em and whispered, "And growing bigger every day."

"I heard that," I groused.

Mama smiled her butter-would-not-melt smile. "I meant for you to hear it, *chérie*. [dear]"

Tante Em pulled out her phone. "Well, I'd better called Ms. Clothilde."

I tried to sit up, but Mama pushed me back down. I tried to ignore the whiff of Chanel *Mademoiselle* and warm memories of home, but my heart clenched. "Why, why would you do that? She's Meauxville's biggest gossip!" My worry about the gossip hid my worry that I might never parent as good as my mama.

"Sweetie, if you think that your pregnancy is not already making the rounds, you're delusional. With Ms. Clothilde in the loop, she'll ensure the gossip doesn't turn vicious."

While Tante Em talked to Ms. Clothilde, I let my mama pamper me a bit — adjusting my pillow, holding my hand, and kissing my forehead. Sometimes, you just need your mama.

Then she opened her mouth. "And who is the daddy of my first grandchild?"

"Umm ... I got a sperm donor." That was my story, not a lie as much as a prevarication. I planned to stick to my story.

The problem with being close with your mama is that she could spot a prevarication from across a football field. As images of my night of 'sperm donation' flooded my memory with Armand's lips, his broad chest, and his touch, my mama watched me carefully.

"Umm-hum." Her lips tightened. A sure sign that she knew I wasn't telling the whole truth. "And what, pray tell, was this sperm donor's name?"

"Sperm donors like to be anonymous." Again, not a lie per se; nevertheless, I avoided eye contact with my mama.

"Umm-hum. Probably for the best. Expect your brothers to ferret your sperm donor out and beat the tar out of him."

I scoffed. Armand was an Army Ranger. Three pissed off Cajun boys would not be an issue for him. Which turned my thoughts yet again to the letter I had sent Armand a month after our encounter. I wrote him that our efforts to give me a child had failed. Not that he responded to that letter — or any other letter I sent him, the *tchu* [ass]. My mama's hand brushed my forehead. As if she could read my mind, her brows drew together, and she bit her bottom lip — just like I did when I'm worried. No wonder she could read my mind. We had the exact same expressions.

"I'll let her know, Ms. Clothilde. That's a good idea." Tante Em clicked off the phone and turned to me. "Ms. Clothilde has an idea that will keep you safe from the attacks that our family has endured and will help you, too."

I shook my head. Ms. Clothilde's machinations were legendary. "Nope."

"Just hear us out ..."

2

Recovery

Armand

Lights out and the lingering smell of sulfur. That's all I remembered. I kept trying to bring it back, but all that would come back to me were the mission plans, jumping from the chopper, and then nothing. A big blank. A big blank that killed two men in my unit and nearly did me in. I heard it was an ambush. The rest of my unit suffered minor injuries, and then there was me. I was surprised to still be alive. Even before the mission, I had a feeling. I expected to die.

Hopped up on pain meds after yet another surgery on my shoulder. The doctor was talking "Blah blah blah ... physical therapy." "Blah blah blah ... use of arm was not 100% and may not ever get there." I registered that last part. He mentioned they had some room at a facility in Louisiana, but I didn't want visitors while I was in a weakened state. I didn't want anyone's pity.

I tried to speak to my doctor. "I don't, don't, don't *veux pas aller en Louisiane* [don't want to go to Louisiana]."

That was when we knew something was wrong with my brain. After conducting multiple tests, the doctors finally identified it as a peculiar brain injury. It didn't affect my understanding, and it didn't seem to affect my French speech, but when I spoke in English, it was a mess. I kept repeating words and simple phrases until I finally gave up and said it in French. Broca's aphasia, they called it. The doctors said it might clear up right away, take months to recover, or I might have it for life. That last one, more than my busted shoulder, would be a career killer.

So, here I was at Walter Reed in Bethesda, thinking I could recover in peace. My physical therapy for the shoulder injury was straight forward. It included exercises, massage, and dry needling. That last therapy hurt like a *putain* but sped up my recovery exponentially. Unlike the work with the physical therapist, my aphasia therapy was slow, incremental, and involved a lot of backtracking.

Dr. Hildago, my bilingual speech and language therapist, used my French, which was unaffected by the damage, to help me regain my spoken English. She seemed impressed with my tortoise-like progress. "You're making great strides."

I shook my head, "I can't, I can't, see it. *Ça m'enerve* [that annoys me]!"

She made some notes in my file. "Trust me. My monolingual patients would kill for your pace of improvement."

The upside of Walter Reed was that it gave me solitude to focus on my recovery. In my distracted brain, only my mom, my emergency contact, knew about my injuries. I smiled at my idiocy when my visitors walked through the door. The thing about Louisiana, and south Louisiana in particular, is there's always someone from Louisiana around. My mother, the traitor, must have hinted to someone about my injury. Word got back home and today I had visitors. *Yippee!*

Unfortunately for my solitude, my good friend, Etienne Benoit, was nearby, doing his FBI training in Quantico. One of a group of four of us that called ourselves the Krewe of Roux. Krewe, because we were a social group (it's a Mardi Gras thing) and roux, because we liked to cook (roux being the essential ingredient in gumbo). Etienne married our good friend and other Krewe member's sister, Angelle, Gelly. She was in D.C. visiting Etienne, and they both decided to visit me.

I hid my aphasia by only speaking in French to them. The moment they arrived, I motioned them out the door to come walk with me. "*Venez avec moi.*"

Etienne was a nosy one. It's why he was going to make a great FBI agent. I wouldn't put it past him to read my chart if we stayed in my room. Evade and escape, that was my plan. Distractions were key.

"*Comment ça se plume ma belle?*" I asked Gelly how she was doing.

My plan worked like gangbusters. Gelly talked all about their life in Meauxville, her plans to open up a second dance school wherever Etienne was stationed, and the success of her Meauxville dance school, *Danse avec moi*. Etienne updated me about his training at Quantico in the FBI and the rest of the Krewe, Beau and Marc, as we walked to the cafeteria for some substandard coffee.

"*Et les autres?*" I filled three cups with the tasteless brew as I angled to hear an update about Renee by asking about everyone else, but Etienne was purposely being obtuse. I had gotten the letter from her letting me know that our attempt to give her a baby had failed. That night was seared into my memory — her light blond locks in my fist, her perfume a field of flowers, her muscular legs pulling me closer, deeper. I had even entertained thoughts of perhaps a few more attempts. But those ideas evaporated once I realized how truly broken I was.

Etienne was too damned observant for his own good. He switched to English. "What others? Let us know who you want to know about, and we'll give you an update." He paid for "coffee" and smirked. The *fils d'putain* was on to me.

I hedged, added sugar and milk in an attempt to make the coffee palatable. "*Je connais pas. Les petits et Renee* [I don't know, the Littles (children in our friend group) and Renee]." Etienne frowned. He was definitely on to me. God dammit, why couldn't I have dull friends?

Gelly, had caught on, at least to my line of questioning, "The children are all doing well. Can't say the same for Renee. She had to take a leave of absence. She's staying with our Mawmaw Babineaux on her farm, *Mes Rêves*. Mawmaw hasn't been feeling well, and she wanted some company."

We sat at one of the tables. Their eyes met. They were, without doubt, holding back on me. "*Pourquoi elle peut pas travailler*? [Why can't she work?]"

Etienne dropped the bomb. "She's pregnant and on restricted activity. She can't stand for long periods, so she can't teach. Plus, she can't be climbing all the stairs at her apartment and Mawmaw's big Acadian house has only one small flight upstairs to the second level. She told everyone she got a sperm donor to give her a baby. The thing is, she's about three months pregnant."

My heart gave a squeeze, and I sprung up, rattling the table and spilling everyone's coffee.

"I knew it. I knew it. You're the 'sperm donor,' aren't you!" Etienne air quoted.

I nodded, "Yes, yes, I, I, I am."

Etienne glared at me and let a few beats pass. He turned to Gelly and back to me. "Enough! Tell us what is wrong!"

I did, and for the next month, Etienne and Gelly worked along with my therapists during their free time to get me back in somewhat working order. The pain, sweat, and frustration were a necessary evil. At first, staying in the Army had been my only goal. Now, I considered that there might be another.

3

Choir Practice

Renee

Choir practice is teacher code for our surreptitious plan to go out for alcoholic libations. This month, choir practice was at Mawmaw Babineaux's farm, *Mes Rêves*. The farm consisted of a large two-story Acadian style house with an expansive front porch, an old barn that needed paint, fields of overgrown gardens, and two goats. We gathered on the front porch to *jaser* [talk/gossip]. *Comme d'habitude* [as usual]. It was the four of us: Shell, Kayleigh, Gelly, and me. Gelly and Etienne were visiting for the weekend from Virginia, where Etienne was training at Quantico. At least I still had friends. With libations and pastries on the side table, we relaxed on rockers and the porch swing. The spring weather was mild, with a warm breeze that spread the scent of honeysuckle from the vines that covered the old barn.

"Mawmaw says she's going to rest and won't be joining us. She also says to have fun, but not too much fun, and if we don't listen to her, to spend the night here," I said.

Shell grimaced with each sip of her herbal tea. "Ahh, I hope she feels better soon. Beau wanted to visit with her when he picks me up."

I snorted. "I'm sure she will scurry out of bed and make Beau some rice and gravy, or whatever else he's hungry for. He's pure gold, according to Mawmaw. The man who single-handedly produced four great grandchildren in less than a year — plus another on the way." I patted Shell's tummy.

Shell pouted. "Hey, I helped."

Kayleigh snickered and sipped her Bayou Rum and diet coke. "You helped adopt the Heberts and cooked little Alex and this new *bébé*. I'm sure you'll get some tertiary acknowledgment." She sighed heavily. "I'm so glad Gelly is back and I'm not the only one imbibing."

Gelly lifted her drink up. "To our lack of pregnancy hormones!"

"Here, here!" Kayleigh snickered, raising her own glass.

Shell and I lifted our herbal teas to toast. "To Gelly and the actual libations, that one day we will drink again." I sniffed the mint and chamomile concoction that Mawmaw had made us. Truth be told, I enjoyed the flavor — unlike Shell, who suffered through her herbal tisanes.

"Did I show y'all my newest creation?" I lifted my wonky, multicolored, crocheted potholder. "Mawmaw is teaching me all her skills!"

Kayleigh's eyes bounced from my potholder to the elegant crocheted doilies on all the side tables. She bit her lower lip. "It's ... a start." I rolled my eyes at the gales of laughter from my so-called friends.

"How's Mawmaw doing? The Littles and Beau are worried about her," Shell asked, trying not to gag on her tea. She was not a fan.

"Considering she has congestive heart failure, she's doing well. The new medicine gives her much more energy. Basically, when I came to live with her, we discussed what she loved doing. She loves cooking, crocheting, and gardening — that's all we do.

And family; she loves to visit with family. She can't walk far, but we help each other to the garden each day."

Gelly frowned. "You, the pregnant woman with activity restrictions, and Mawmaw with heart problems, help each other down the steps to the garden. Y'all need more help?"

"We have a ramp and we don't walk that far. It's not like I'm teaching on my feet all day. Our limitations match. For the moment, it works out well."

Shell's cup clinked when she set her tea down. "I think you need more help and also protection."

I peered out at the garden. My brothers Eric and Jeb were there today. "I don't think protection is a problem. My brothers are taking shifts watching us."

Shell shook her head. "Is that a sustainable solution?"

I shook my head. "Nope." Inhaling, I savored my herbal tea and let the chamomile calm me as I stared out at the empty field. "I think I've taken enough from my family. I can't ask my brothers to guard me forever."

Shell frowned. "You haven't asked anything of your family. You were perfectly content to try to go this alone. They pushed their way in. I know how Ms. Clothilde railroaded you into coming over her and helping Mawmaw."

"I'm grateful she did, but I won't ask my family to do more." I closed my eyes and rocked in my chair, the familiar squeak of wood whispering, *You're home.*

Shell reached over and clasped my hand. "I'm not talking about family. I think you need a caretaker to tend the gardens, run y'all's errands, and provide security. Someone who lives on the property. Isn't there an old run-down apartment in the barn for the old ranch manager?"

"Shell," I scoffed, "nearly all my friends have abandoned me because I'm a 'fallen woman' and you want me to hire some man to spend the night out here? You think I'm persona non grata now? Just wait until after that."

"Screw them," Kayleigh said. "What's more important is that you're safe, rested, and worry free."

Shell perked up. "We can use that service that I used to find Beau. That worked out well for me!" She patted her tummy.

I focused on Shell's tummy and then raised my teacher's eyebrow. "I'm pretty sure the hiring service did not have the services Beau provides in mind. At least, they can't legally advertise that." Shell threw a napkin at me, and I lobbed it back. "Look, we just need some help around the farm. I don't need a man."

"Of course not!" Gelly said. "Plus, there is your sperm donor to think of."

Shell picked up that baton. "Yes, let's discuss the sperm donor."

"Let's not." I bit into one of the scones on the side table as a distraction. "Mmm. You should try one of these. Delicious. Try the blueberry, for sure."

Shell continued, as if she hadn't heard me. "I thought you still had like a year to save before you could afford that sperm donation procedure."

"I got lucky, I ... uh... came into some money." I held out my scone to her. "Want a bite?"

Kayleigh shook her head and tsked. "You suck at lying Renee."

I glanced at my wrist, my empty wrist. "Well, would you look at that? Tempus fugit, I think it's time for my nap."

"Tempus fugit, indeed, and time is passing you by as you lie to your best friends. Sperm donor's name, please." Gelly snapped her fingers.

"It's not just my secret." I hid my face in my hand, my fingers rubbing circles between my eyebrows.

"As long as we are all aware that there is a secret lurking in our friendship," Kayleigh said.

"Hold on," Shell said, her eyes scrolling up as she considered. Thinking aloud, she added, "We don't have to ask Renee to reveal anything. We can figure this out. The deed probably wasn't done here. Meauxville has eyes and ears everywhere. And Renee hasn't been anywhere in months."

Kayleigh's eyes brightened. "Three months exactly. Renee, how many months along are you? That isn't anyone else's secret, right?"

I heaved a sigh. "Three months."

Kayleigh nodded. "Gelly's wedding. So, there was only one time that I remember when you weren't hanging out with us. That was after the wedding reception. When ..." My eyes met Kayleigh's. "Oh, my God, Armand! When Armand walked us from the reception to our rooms to make sure we got there safely, he dropped me off first."

Shell whistled. "That is some prime grade A sperm."

My mouth dropped open. "Shell, you're married!"

"But not blind. And what has our dear Armand said about the baby?"

"I sent him a letter in January. My dot arrived, and I let him know he was off the hook. Not that he thought he would raise Junior here with me. I mailed and emailed him over and over again once I realized my mistake. I wanted to see how he was and to divulge my change of status, but I didn't get a reply or phone call or anything." I patted my belly. "His letters came back 'return to sender.'"

"That fiend!" Kayleigh stood, nearly tipping over her rocker.

"No, he was worried about his last mission. He made me fill out some paperwork. I guess to make sure if there was a child it would get benefits. Anyway, after that he ghosted me. Since no one has said anything, I figured he was done with his good deed for the year. I wanted to raise this child on my own, anyway."

"That still what you want?" Kayleigh asked.

Tears welled in my eyes. Stupid eyes. Stupid hormones. "Absolutely! Besides, I'm not sure I get a choice. Armand gave me radio silence."

Shell grasped my hands. "I was planning on telling you both tonight, but it seems I need to do it sooner rather than later."

"What's up?" Kayleigh asked, glancing over at Shell and my hands.

"First, let me tell you both, he's ok." I inhaled sharply. "Armand was wounded about two months ago. Only his mother knew because those were his stated wishes. She let a clue drop when the Krewe visited her asking about Armand, because they hadn't heard from him. Gelly and Etienne went and checked on him at Walter Reed. They said he has some issues to work through but overall is in good health."

I squeezed her hand. "How long has he been there?"

"Since radio silence, since January," Shell answered, shaking her head at my brothers, who noticed my distress and were heading up to fix things.

"So, he might not have gotten my first message? Why didn't they tell me immediately?" I stood up and started pacing the front porch. "Stupid, hard-headed men. They think they know better. Patting us on our heads and telling us not to worry our pretty heads."

"Uh, Renee," Shell said, but Kayleigh touched her hand and shook her head. Knowing me well, Eric and Jeb took one look at me and scurried out of range. Or, at least, they tried.

I grabbed up the scones first. They had a nice throwing heft. "Stupid," I launched a scone at Jeb. "Arrogant," I launched another at Eric, "men." This time, my aim was true. The scone hit Jeb, who had moved into range dodging the first scone.

"Hey, what did I do?" Jeb complained, brushing off his chest where the scone had struck and grimaced at the chocolate stain on his shirt.

I sniffed. "You have a Y chromosome, so you're guilty by default." I turned back around.

Eric, the idiot, called, "Five-second rule," and picked up his blueberry scone, laughing. "You're slow. You knew what was coming. She is and always will be Renee 'The Fireball' Babineaux." Eric teased.

Shell put her hands up. "Don't kill the messenger. Beau didn't want to tell you because of your condition." I lifted an eyebrow and glared at Shell's baby bump. "Well, he can't keep secrets from me. Also, we didn't know your 'close' connection to Armand." She air-quoted the close.

"Whatever! Tell me everything!" I demanded.

And Shell spilled about the injury, the surgeries, and how he was in rehab. She didn't know the specifics, but at least I now knew he was alive and wasn't ghosting me.

"So, you gonna let him know?" Gelly asked.

I shook my head. "Let's wait until I'm off restricted activity. After that, I'll let him know. Let him focus on his recovery for now."

4

Krewe of Roux

Armand

My shoulder felt almost back to normal, with just a hint of lingering soreness. In contrast, despite improvement, my speech was still not sufficient to resume duty. Silver lining, my progress prevented a medical discharge. Dr. Hildalgo had been working with Melodic Intonation Therapy. My comprehension in both languages and my fluency in French were unimpaired, thus I just needed to work on speaking English. Singing, rather than speaking, was working wonders. I could pretty much hide my issues from most people. My problems persisted only under stressful conditions. Dr. Hidalgo was continuing the therapy via a computer program and tele-visits with her. So, I was officially discharged from the Military Advanced Training Center, or MATC. I had six months to get back in combat condition. I headed back home to Meauxville to see Renee about our child.

The entire Krewe knew I'd be heading back. Before I left, Etienne tried to talk me out of banging on Renee's door the instant I arrived in Meauxville. Caving to the pressure, I spent my first night with the rest of the Krewe at Beau and Shell's house. After catching up with the Littles, which now included

Beau and Shell's four children and Marc's Sofia, I was ready for adult time. Beau fired up the pit, and as wood smoke scented the air, we each grabbed a cold beer and started catching up.

"I'm going to crash here tonight if that's okay with you." I raised my chin in question, and Beau just nodded. I figured I needed to cool my jets before I spoke with Renee.

"You'll be on the couch. I'm running out of bedrooms." Beau smiled, leaned back in his chair, and took a swig of his beer.

Marc threw some ice from the cooler at him. "You *are* out of bedrooms. We need to add some more room to your house if you keep adding kids at this breakneck speed."

Beau grinned and raised his hands. "Hey! Three of them were adoptions."

I snickered, "And, two, two were made the old-fashioned way." I was getting better, but it still annoyed me when I doubled words.

The Krewe either didn't notice or didn't care. Beau shrugged. "I always wanted a big family."

Marc chuckled. "Now you can achieve your goal of running the farm without expending any energy."

We sat back and enjoyed the cloudless night sky. I pondered family. I smiled, imagining Renee, a Valkyrie, protecting her child, our child. *Our child*. My heart tripped. Why hadn't she told me? *Calm, stay calm*. First, I needed to see and speak with Renee. Then I would tackle the uncomfortable discussion with my mother.

Marc broke the silence first. "You know, if you need a place to stay, you could see if you can rent the room above the Au Bal dress shop. Renee is no longer renting there."

"I don't think Armand will be staying there," Etienne said. "He has another place in mind."

Clearly, Etienne had not divulged my secrets.

"Where would that be?" Beau asked.

"I'm going to head over to *Mes Rêves*," I mumbled, and took a longer swig of my beer.

"What's that?" Beau asked. Sensing trouble, he set his beer down.

"He said he's going to head over to your Mawmaw Babineaux's farm, *Mes Rêves*." Marc cocked his head to the side and frowned. "Why would you stay there?"

Understanding struck, and Beau straightened out of his Adirondack chair so abruptly that the chair fell over. Before the chair hit the ground, he had stomped over to me. "You *fils d'putain*! The wedding!" He grabbed me up by the shoulders.

"What's going on over there?" Shell asked from the porch.

"Nothing, dear." Beau called and pushed me back into my chair. In a growled whisper, he said, "Explain yourself now. That's my cousin. My outcast cousin, who has basically been rejected by many of her so-called friends because of this pregnancy. This better be good."

I held my hands up. "I did it to protect, protect her."

Marc took a gulp of his beer and slowly shook his head. "That was not the right thing to say, bro."

"I agree with Marc," Shell commented from the porch.

"Can you *not* listen to this?" I called over to Shell.

"Not gonna happen," Shell and Beau said in unison.

"I'm telling you, man. She was going to get some rando to impregnate her. Beau, she was going to use some stranger's sperm and spend all her money doing it."

Beau's hold of me let up. "What are you talking about? Renee wouldn't do that."

Shell called down to them from the porch, "Yes, she would. She was saving up for a sperm donor. That's how we figured out it was Armand."

"You knew!" Beau turned to his wife on the porch.

"I was giving Armand a day to fess up," Shell retorted.

"Can I fess, fess up in private, please?" I asked, massaging my temples, as Beau and the rest of the Krewe hovered over me.

Shell rolled her eyes, grabbed her hated herbal tea, and headed inside. "Fine, but don't screw it up." Shell flounced into the house, leaving me with a furious Beau.

Beau didn't back down and crossed his arms over his chest. "I'm waiting."

Marc, pretending to eat popcorn, whispered, "Me, too." Etienne bit his lip and shook his head.

"Like Sh … Shell said, she was saving money for a sperm donor. Her biological clock was ticking and, according to her, all, all the guys she met were worthless losers. I was leaving, and I had a bad feeling about, about the mission."

"What? You were just going to leave her with a kid and forget it?" Beau was not warming up to my explanation.

I shook my head. "No, I had her sign forms. She was given power of attorney and if anything happened to me, she would have gotten all my death benefits."

Beau shook his head. "Nice try, Armand. She can't get widow's benefits if she's not your widow."

The silence after that statement was deafening.

Marc whistled. "What exactly did you do, Armand?"

I pressed my lips together and then explained. "Did you know that in Texas, military personnel can get a proxy wedding?"

Etienne, who had been staying out of it, took a swig of his brew and said, "You're toast!"

"I second Etienne!" Shell yelled through the living room window. "You have one day to tell her, Armand!"

Marc grinned. "Ears like a bat. My friends, we have a wedding to celebrate." He handed us each a fresh ice cold LA31 beer.

Beau took the beer, but didn't appear convinced. He pressed his lips together, then said, "You're shitting me? Does Renee know that she's married?"

I shrugged. "Not unless she carefully read the stack of paperwork I sent her. I told her they were to make sure if we did make a kid and if I died, that the kid would be taken care of."

Etienne snorted. "Forgetting to let her know that she was signing a marriage document?"

Beau smirked. "Your ass is toast! Welcome to the family!"

Shell yelled from the window, "Now, you need to go over there and help out Renee. Her brothers are there, but you need to make sure she doesn't overdo it. She's supposed to be on restricted activity, because of her blood pressure, but she's not slowing down. She's trying to get that farm up and running for Mawmaw Babineaux."

"Her blood pressure is high? I knew she was on restricted activity, but isn't high blood pressure bad bad when you're pregnant?"

Shell called back. "She has gestational hypertension. She developed it earlier than most pregnant women usually get it. It's another reason why she isn't teaching and why she can't live in the apartment over the Au Bal dress shop. Of course, she decided to live upstairs at *Mes Rêves*."

"What? Why would she do that? What did the doctor say? Is she ok?"

Shell, tired of yelling, returned to the porch. "She's fine, but sometimes she overdoes it. She needs some help."

I got up to leave and stomped over to my Challenger.

"Where ya goin'?" Beau asked as I headed out.

I pulled out my keys and unlocked the car door. "To let Renee know that I will be around to help."

"Beware the ogres at the gate!" Marc yelled to my back.

I turned and asked, "Who?"

Marc grinned. "Her brothers have been camping out each night watching over her."

Shell cocked her head. "I thought her brothers went home at night."

"Renee is touchy about needing help, so they guard her on the down low." Marc said. "I know because they asked for pointers about patrolling and staying out of sight. They have everything covered. I think tonight is Kevin's turn."

I got in my car and rolled down the window. "The Babineaux guards will have to learn to deal with me." I started up the Challenger and put her in gear.

"If they don't kill you first," Etienne yelled before I sped down the driveway.

5

Some 'splaining to Do

Renee

I had just laid down on the downstairs couch, my impromptu bed, when someone started pounding on the front door.

Mawmaw called from her room. "Renee, *chérie,* can you see who's making that racket?"

I peeked through the side window and saw Armand pounding on the door. "Open this door right now, now, Renee. You have some some 'splaining to, to do!" *Gah! Mr. Tall, Dark, and Angry.*

Looks like someone spilled the beans. As I slid the bolt over, Kevin, my overprotective brother, rather, one of my overprotective brothers, came running up the porch. Kevin grabbed Armand by the shoulders, and before Armand, a six-foot something Army Ranger, could maim my brother, I stepped in. "Kevin! What are you doing here?"

"Watching over you, Renee. After the attacks, Beau told us that everyone in his circle needs protection and it's not like Mawmaw could protect you."

"I don't need protection from Armand. Go back to wherever you were lurking." *Overprotective, overbearing, big brothers. Why was I cursed to be a baby sister to three Neanderthals?*

Kevin shook his chestnut curls. "Nope." He glared at Armand. "First, you tell me why you're angry with my baby sister. You know the one on bedrest that should not have any stress in her life. Don't get me wrong. I'm sure you're in the right, but no one messes with my sister, but me, Jeb, and Eric." With that, my idiot brother got into Armand's face.

I cocked my head to the side and folded my arms in front of me. "First of all, I'm on restricted activity, not bed rest. *Je suis pas en sucre.* Stop treating me like I'm made of glass. Let's talk about stress. How about the stress caused by my brother threatening to beat up a good friend in front of me?"

Armand snorted, "He, he could try."

"Both of you stand down. Armand, good to see you. I'm glad you've recovered from your injuries. Will you be heading back to your Ranger unit soon?" I gave him a big hug. His muscles were tight, but I held him until I felt him relax against me.

Kevin mumbled, "Thanks for your service." Which made Armand squirm and made me fight a smile.

I turned to my brother. "Kevin, I'm fine and safe. Let me catch up with my friend. Are you staying in the barn? You know there is a studio apartment there." I pointed to Mawmaw's run down barn. "It's not fancy, but if you, Jeb, and Eric insist on watching over us, you'd be more comfortable there."

This time it was Kevin's turn to show the *tête dure* [hard-headed] Babineaux spirit. "I can't watch over the house from there." He folded his arms in front of him, not budging.

Armand interrupted just before I could argue with him. "Richard Security, Marc's company, will be installing security tomorrow. I'll get you, your brothers, and Beau a feed."

"Excuse me?!" I said, while Kevin grinned.

Then Kevin fist bumped Armand and said, "Thanks, man." He trotted down the porch steps.

"Gotta keep the womenfolk safe!" Armand added, just to annoy me.

"Get in here before I decide to take a broom to both of you," I said, and pulled him into the foyer.

Inside the foyer, I scanned Armand for any sign of injuries. He looked perfect — tall, dark, and perfect. *Damn my pregnancy hormones.* "Let's go to the parlor and talk ... quietly, Mawmaw is resting."

When we got to the parlor, I sat down, but Armand paced. He stopped pacing to glare at me. "Why, why didn't you tell me? You were, you were supposed to tell me. Why, why did you tell me you weren't pregnant?"

I stood up. "Ah! You did get my first letter." I left the room to rummage in my backpack in the foyer.

He followed me out. "What are you doing?"

I grabbed hold of the package of letters and threw each one at him. "Return to sender!" I winged another one at him. "Return to sender." Then another, until he grabbed the rest of them from me. "I tried to tell you; you wouldn't read or even open any of my letters!" And then it came, the telltale sign I was getting worked up. "Oh, shit!" I rushed to the bathroom, slammed the door, and lost what little I had managed to eat that night. A stellar exit scene, Renee.

"Renny, Renny are, are you, you okay?" Armand called through the door. I heard it then. The repetition. *Something's wrong* flickered through my brain. Then I was sick again.

After cleaning up, I opened the door and saw that Mawmaw had woken up and lured Armand away from the bathroom door. Thank God for her homemade rice and gravy. Kevin also sat at her table, shoveling food into his mouth. She was offering them some pecan pie and Blue Bell homemade vanilla ice cream when I walked in.

"Renee dear, do you want some ice cream as well?" She knew it eased the burning and was already dishing the dessert into bowls when I responded. She nodded towards the pie slices she just plated.

"Yes, ma'am." I served the men their pie, and they dug in as I sprinkled crushed salty tortilla chips on my bowl.

Kevin smirked. "Wow, you just have all the symptoms."

I shot him the finger when Mawmaw turned her head. Kevin chortled, and the corner of Armand's mouth crooked up.

"Mrs. Babineaux," Armand started.

"Now *chéri*, you know I told you to call me Mawmaw. You've been friends with Beau and these ruffians for forever." She pointed to Kevin and Renee.

"Hey, I'm not a ruffian." I stopped inhaling my ice cream for a moment to grouse.

"Ferdinand," was all Mawmaw said, and Kevin burst out in gales of laughter.

I pouted. "I was misled by a book! That's not my fault."

"I never heard this story!" Armand complained.

Mawmaw patted his back. "We were afraid that dear Angelle, who was Renee's mini-me, would copy her, so we kept it under wraps."

Armand turned to me and said, "Spill!"

I put my elbow on the table and my chin in my hand. "Have you ever read *Ferdinand the Bull*?"

"I'm Bailey Marie's *parrain* [godfather], so only like a million times." Armand told me.

I sipped the cool water that Mawmaw handed me. "Well, there you go. Anyway, when I was seven, I thought it was more of a non-fiction story."

"Holy shit, Diable, you tried to make friends with Diable!?" Kevin snorted with laughter and Armand elbowed him hard. "Where the hell were you when she was trying to make friends with a homicidal bull?"

Kevin raised his hands. "Hey, I'm the one that ran into the field and dragged her out of danger." Armand shook his head and pushed away his pie. Kevin snatched it up.

Armand's gaze returned to Mawmaw. "As I was saying," Armand continued, "who, who is helping you out? I saw chickens and a, a garden, and it looks like you need some, some help."

There it was again. That repetition. It didn't look like anyone else had noticed it.

"We have Kevin, Jeb, and Eric who help out some," Mawmaw told him. "But I know they're busy and just helping out an old woman."

"We love you, Mawmaw, and we're happy to help when we can," Kevin assured her, and leaned over to kiss her on the cheek.

Armand continued, "I noticed that Renee answered the door. Isn't she supposed to be on bedrest?"

"Restricted activity," I informed the room. Not that anyone was listening to me.

Kevin stiffened. "We can't do everything!"

Armand raised his dark eyebrows. "My point exactly. You can't can't do everything. I can help."

Mawmaw also got defensive. "She told us she's been feeling better and hasn't been spotting since the first time and that Fast Clinic doctor told her she can walk 20 minutes a day. It's just about the time for our evening walk, but I'm tired today."

"No criticism intended. I'm, I'm just offering my services. I can stay here and help you while I finish my recovery. That way, Kevin, Eric, and Jeb only need to head over when I have to go in for my doctors' appointments."

Kevin mulled it over as he chewed. Then he swallowed. "It would be nice to have some free time."

"Where would you stay?" Mawmaw asked.

"In the house, that way I can be on hand when you need anything like opening jars, getting things off top shelves, or even harvesting your garden." He gave her his charming spider to the fly grin.

"That would be nice." Mawmaw bit her lip, as though she were actually contemplating it.

I stood up. "Really! Because my reputation isn't besmirched enough. I need to put living in sin on the list of my transgressions." I started cleaning up the kitchen.

"Renee Geneviève Babineaux! You stop that talk. If I'm here, I assure you there will be no sinning, at least not of the kind you're referring."

Armand shook his head. "Of course not, Mawmaw. I just want to help and, since I'm recovering, I need a place to stay. I can help you take care of everything and also help keep everyone safe."

Mawmaw hugged Armand. "It would give the boys a well-deserved break. They haven't been able to do much except work and watch over us."

Armand got up and started drying the dishes that I washed. "And I can help with chores or whatever you need fixed around the house. I can even pay rent."

"You will do no such thing," Mawmaw told him. "You're an honorary grandson, and Renee actually hasn't been feeling well, no matter what that doctor said."

"Mawmaw! I'm fine." Actually, the doctor had said that he wasn't a specialist, but from what he could tell, I was fine. At this point, that was all I needed to know.

"Renee, *chérie*, you can barely keep any food down. You've lost weight when you should be gaining weight, and you still haven't been to a real obstetrician."

I grabbed a basket from beside the kitchen door. "I can't help it. I can't afford the premiums. I'm not talking about this now. I'm going to go and harvest from the garden."

Armand took a second basket and followed me out. Mawmaw called out to him as we went outside, "Don't let her carry anything, Armand. I keep insisting, but you know the *tête dure* Babineaux."

Armand turned and smiled, "I'm familiar with the, the breed." Kevin's laugh followed him out.

Armand had picked up a second basket. I'm sure our weedy little garden underwhelmed him. Tough. It was all we could do and my brothers had zero interest in farming, so it was up to me. I kneeled and started harvesting the lettuce and the collard greens. The scent of the dirt calmed my stomach and my nerves while the breeze brought the scent of rain. He kneeled beside me to help.

When I was sure we were alone and wouldn't be overheard, I turned to him. "So, what happened? You look like you're whole and hale, but something is off. Can you talk about it?"

He shrugged. "I'm actually not sure. I was, was on that mission. The one I told you about."

I kept my tone steady. "The one you thought would be your last mission?"

"Yes, yes, we landed, and then everything went black. Then yada yada yada, here I am."

I shook my head. "Nice try. What happened? You did get my first letter, right?"

He cut some more greens in silence and then said quietly, "The one where you said you weren't pregnant. Yes, I did. Why, why did you tell me that?"

"At the time, it was true. I got my period, and I thought there was no child. How was I to know that early on you can get a light one, even though you're pregnant?" I patted my stomach. "Now, I know."

"And after that? You could have texted me."

"My life turned into a storm when I found out I was pregnant. I went on restricted activity, had to move, and had to take unpaid maternity leave from my job. We're only given twenty days. After that, I used my ten days of sick leave. After that, I was scrambling to find inexpensive doctors because I couldn't afford to keep my health insurance. Plus, you returned the rest of my letters unopened. I thought you were ghosting me. Now tell me what happened." I looked around for the stool I normally used to rest.

Armand, sensing my need, found the stool. I sat as he continued with his story. I think it helped that he wasn't facing me. "There was an ambush. My, my team was hit. We lost two good men. I was hurt, and and in and out of surgery and recovery. Mostly head, head trauma, although my shoulder was also hurt and required surgery. The other injuries were not career-threatening."

"But your shoulder is?"

Armand shook his head. "It could have been but, when I thought there was no baby, I focused on rehab to try to save my career. Rehabbing the shoulder has been pretty seamless."

I frowned at him. "That's why you returned my other letters?" Armand shook his head. "There is something else. Something about your speech."

Armand nodded. We gathered our baskets, or rather Armand gathered them and walked in silence as the spring sunset. At the first mosquito, we headed back to the screened porch. Kevin texted that since Armand was there, he was taking off for the night. Upon our return, Mawmaw told us she was tired. I gave her a hug and told her I loved her.

"Is she doing okay?" Armand asked as we walked to the parlor to talk. I shook my head and tears welled in my eyes. I was horrified when one slipped out. Stupid, stupid hormones. Armand pulled me in for a hug. Normally, I tower over men, but with him, I could lay my head on his shoulder. I remember that about him from our one time. "It's okay, *chérie*,"

I shook my head against his shoulder. "It's not. She's dying. I don't think she will make it to Junior's birth."

I could feel Armand's smile against my head. "Junior, that's what you're calling him?"

I nodded. "Mawmaw has been trying to figure out his daddy's name. She will no doubt start calling him Armand Junior starting tomorrow morning. Be prepared for everyone to know."

"The Krewe, the Krewe knows."

I took a deep breath. "I told Shell, hoping she could break it gently to them. I was just trying to keep you from getting beat up."

Armand's chest rumbled with mirth. "Not sure if you have accomplished that. Beau, Beau appeared pretty pissed off. Also, your brothers are going to kill me."

I shook my head again. "Not if I tell them. It was my idea."

With a grin, Armand pulled back and gazed at me. "It's, it's funny that you think that will make a difference." He eased me onto the parlor sofa next to him, stared into my eyes, and took a deep breath. "This is our child."

Shaking my head again, I reminded him, "This is my child. I make the decisions. Remember, you didn't want anything to do with a child."

He lifted his hand and cupped my face. "No, I was just pretty sure I was going to die and wanted you to have what you so desperately wanted. I just wanted to make you happy, Renny. Plus, I knew if you raised my child, it would be raised well."

I sobbed. Ugh, hormones. He pulled me into a hug and I soaked his shirt in tears. After a moment, our eyes met. "What now?"

He smiled and handed me a handkerchief. "Now, we have a baby? We need to talk, work out logistics. Why don't we go for breakfast tomorrow?"

I wiped my tears away. "Bad idea. Breakfast is usually followed by a vomit fest, which is why I only eat toast and tea. How about later in the morning? After that, I can eat about anything. You might want to go to a buffet. Junior here is an eater. Mawmaw said she's so happy I'm here because I'm eating all her old canned foods. She was afraid she would have to will them to someone. I'm basically an eating machine. I don't know why I'm not gaining weight."

"We'll get you a better doctor, and I'll get you whatever you want for breakfast. Let's just talk. We will figure it all out, Renny, I promise. Let me run and get my things. Lock the door. I'll be back in under ten minutes."

$$6$$

Kill You Dead

Armand

T he scowl Beau gave me as I returned promised retribution. Like I told Renee, it did not matter that it was a joint decision. He crossed his hands over his chest as I packed up my things. "So, everything resolved?"

I shrugged. "No, but I'm spending the night there tonight, and then we're going out for an early lunch."

Beau moved closer. His buzz cut was gone, but he was still 100% Marine. His voice was deadly soft as he got in my face. "When you will let her know that you married her?"

I nodded, "That we have a marriage license on record, yes. I don't know if that counts as being married."

"Does the Army consider you married?" I nodded, and he whacked me on the back. "Well, there you go. That means that you need to let her know. Shell wants to let her know tonight. I held her off saying it was your mess, and you needed to clean it up, Rule 43." He cuffed me in the back of the head. "Do better or expect my wrath."

"Your wrath might need to wait in line behind your cousins." I rubbed the back of my head. "Hey you know I had a brain injury, right?" I grabbed my stuff and headed out.

Beau grinned. "That was months ago. Toughen up, buttercup. You wanna chill before you head back over there?"

I shook my head. "Naw, Kevin took off, so I need to get back right away. He seemed happy for the help. However, once word gets out, I have a feeling I will be fending off your Babineaux cousins."

"Not making a lot of fans here, are you? Welcome home, you idiot!" Beau gave me a side hug and whacked my back.

"Thanks for holding Shell off. I appreciate the help, man."

Beau guffawed. "Don't thank me. I'm still planning to beat the shit outta you. I'm just waiting for things to die down and for you to get your feet under you."

I rolled my eyes and headed toward my car. "Now that the cat is out of the bag, I need to call my mom. She might not leave enough of me for any Babineaux to beat up. When she's done, there might be nothing left but smoke and cinders. I can't imagine how having a grandchild will cut into her love lives."

Beau snorted as he walked beside me. "FYI, that woman is NOT babysitting my cousin."

"Junior will probably be your godchild."

Beau nodded. "You owe me one. It's a boy?"

I got in my car and rolled down the window. "We don't know. We need to get Renee to a real obstetrician using my benefits. Mawmaw Babineaux has taken to calling him Junior. Although, soon she will be calling him Armand Junior; hence, my need to call my mom. That news will fly like the wind in Meauxville."

"It's probably already old news. Wait until you take Renee out to eat. You'll know then if everyone knows." I grimaced and Beau patted my shoulder. "G'night man."

"Night. Give Shell a big, wet kiss for me." I smirked at him as I found my keys.

"You wish. You have enough female problems." Beau smirked. "A rooster one day and a feather duster the next. How far you have fallen."

I chuckled. "Being a father is not a fall, as you know. Just a different path." Beau smacked my car hood and returned to his family. I turned the ignition and scanned the night sky. Recognizing Polaris, the North Star, I reflected on how it had guided sailors and runaway slaves to safety. I wished I had a guide in these rough waters. As I drove, I inhaled the fresh air streaming in from the windows and had Siri dial my mother, who picked up on the fourth ring.

"Hey, Mom. I have some news."

"Hold on, Armand, let me move to the next room." The way she whispered let me know she had company. "Ok hon, what's up?"

Pull the Band-Aid off. "I just wanted to let you know before the news hit town. I'm ... I'm having a baby."

"What? Who?" she sputtered.

"My, my friend, Renee." I turned on to Highway 31 to head to Mawmaw's farm.

"Your friend Renee, Renee Babineaux. Word was she got a sperm donor because she wanted a kid."

"She did, that that would be me." The line went silent. "Mom, you still there?"

"I'm going to kill you dead." I pulled off the road so I could pay attention to the scolding my mama was about to inflict on me.

"Mama."

"Don't you mama me. Dead. What were you thinking? You weren't thinking at all, that's what it was. What kind of hair-brained scheme? *Couillon, imbecile, idiot*!"

That didn't seem fair. "Excuse me? Aren't you all about free love?"

"Yes, I am of the mind of why buy the whole hog when you can get the sausage for free—"

"—Ugh! Mom! TMI! —"

"—Except I'm more about being a responsible partner. How could you not use protection?"

"Like you did with my sperm donor?" I ill-advisedly asked.

"Don't throw this back on me. I was a 16-year-old kid, and I don't regret what happened because it gave me you. Not that you won't be the death of me with your injuries — and now this surprise."

I pulled back on the road because I could hear in her voice that her rant was winding down. "We don't regret it either. We were both clean and Renee wanted a baby. Getting a rando sperm donor was a terrible idea."

Mama humphed. "So, you decided to simply gift her with a baby and then thought that would be the end."

My breath expelled with a deep sigh. This conversation was not getting easier. "I didn't really think it all through. I was deploying."

After a few ticks of silence, Mama exploded. "*Mon Dieu*! You thought you were going to die. You did this because you thought that would be your last mission."

My lips pinched together. "It almost was."

In the silence, I could nearly feel Mama shaking her head. "So dead. I am going to kill you so dead. I can't believe you didn't talk this over with me."

"I was holding my tongue. I had a bad feeling, but I didn't want to tell anyone."

I heard the soft banging. My mama, more than anyone, missed landlines and being able to smash down phones in anger. The banging was her softly whacking the phone on a table. "And how—" frustration etched in each word as she picked her phone back up, "—how were you going to let me know that I had a grandchild, if you were gone? You left that up to her to tell me?"

I chewed on my lower lip. "Did I mention that I didn't think things through?" The banging resumed, only this time much louder. I was probably going to have to buy her another phone after this.

She got back on the line. "Come over in the morning."

Remembering my last awkward morning at her apartment, I asked, "Will you be alone?"

She was silent, then said, "Come over at ten."

I pulled into Mawmaw Babineaux's drive. "I can't. I'm taking Renee for an early lunch then."

"Fine, come by after. No excuses! As soon as you finish speaking to her, you come by here! *Tu comprends?*"

"*Oui, maman*, I understand." Because there was no way to refuse.

7

Charming Mawmaw

Renee

Armand knocked on the spare bedroom door at 10 am. I wasn't feeling well after my morning bout. I was lying in bed with a cool, wet washcloth over my face. "Come in," I called out because I couldn't make it to the door.

In two steps, he was beside my bed. "Are, are you okay?"

"Just feeling a little ill. It should pass." I remained still, having learned long ago that movement made me queasier.

Brushing aside the washcloth, he felt my forehead for fever. "Do we need to, to go to the doctor?"

"No need. Mawmaw brought me a tray with mint tea and saltines." Picking up the tray I'd had been balancing on my stomach, I placed it on the night table.

Armand guided the tray placement and helped me get seated and comfortable on the bed.

Mawmaw called up the stairs. "Armand, help her down those stairs. She insisted I take the downstair bedroom, but even that Fast Clinic doctor said she shouldn't be taking the stairs."

Armand frowned at that, so I distracted him. "I need my robe and then only slow movements. Fast ones summon the vomit monster."

Armand fetched my robe and helped me into it. Then he tenderly wrapped his arms around my back. I could smell his cologne, the familiar scent of vetiver. I inhaled deeply. From there, we plodded down the stairs. Armand supported me as we moved down the stairs to the makeshift bed in the parlor.

It was too comforting. I didn't trust the feeling. "I'm fine now, really." I shook him off as I sat down.

He called toward the kitchen once he had me situated. "Does, does this happen to her often?"

"Often enough," Mawmaw said. She had shuffled into the foyer, her grey curls wild around her head, and dressed in a pink 1970s muumuu with a big white floral print. She had a bottle of ginger ale to help me out.

Armand took the bottle from her, kissed her cheek, and opened it before he handed it to me. "Drink."

I would have argued, except I loved ginger ale. It always made me feel better. Even a small sniff of it calmed my nerves and my stomach. Argue later, sip now.

"I should, should probably move into Renee's room." Armand said.

"No, that would be living in sin, and you'll not live in sin in my house. I don't think so. She sometimes sleeps in the parlor to avoid the stairs. You can move a cot into the pantry right next to the parlor. Then you can get her hot tea, saltines, and ginger ale when she needs them." She shuffled toward the door that connected the parlor to the pantry, opening it to show how it connected to the kitchen.

Armand nodded. "That works for me. It's your house, Ms. Babineaux. You know best."

"I told you to call me Mawmaw." She shuffled past Armand, and he leaned down and gave her a peck on her cheek. She grinned at that and raised her eyebrows to me. Our eyes were the exact same ice blue color. Great, Mawmaw is smitten with him.

Armand nodded at Mawmaw Babineaux and asked if he could speak to her in the kitchen. I considered protesting, but by then I was too tired. Before he left, Armand checked the temperature of the ginger ale and tucked a throw around me. Feeling warm and cozy, I sipped my cold ginger ale and wondered what Armand was up to. Mawmaw would put him in his place. Of that, I was sure. I grinned and finished up my drink. My stomach grumbled softly for food.

When they came back, Mawmaw beamed adoringly at Armand. *WTF?* Armand reached out onto the porch and pulled in his duffle bag. He carried it across the living room as he explained how things would be.

"After, after lunch, I'll get some more supplies and head back here. Your brothers will be guarding the house while we go and eat. Then, I'll be bunking next door to you, Renee. I'll, I'll be here to help from when you wake up until you go to sleep."

Too bad he won't be in my bed. Bad Renee! Images of Armand, naked and over me, flitted through my brain. Nope, that's what got me into this mess. *Not that you're a mess*, I told Junior, patting my stomach. I looked down to hide my blush. Raising my eyes, I noticed that Armand's eye landed on my hand. Was that a smile?

The hunger came, as it always did, after my stomach calmed. My stomach growled loudly.

Armand grinned, "Hungry? C'mon, c'mon, let's get you two some food." He turned to Mawmaw. "I'll be out with her for a couple of hours, but she'll be mostly sitting." He held my arm like an invalid as he led me to his car.

"I think I'm almost through the worst of it. I have an appointment with an OB-GYN at the free clinic in two weeks."

"Why, why the free clinic? You said earlier you can't afford your premiums, but I thought one of the few financial benefits of teaching was good health insurance."

"I went on a leave without pay, which will end in July, and Principal James said that after that I will *not* be rehired. You know, because I'm a fallen woman. He said there was a moral turpitude clause in our contracts, which means that I won't have insurance for the birth. I didn't want to start with an OB-GYN that I'd have to give up."

He helped me get into the car, saying, "That, that won't be an issue," before shutting the door and jogging around to the driver's side.

I furrowed my brow. What did he mean by that?

8

Brunch Confessional

Armand

I debated, as we drove to town, how I would inform Renee that she was legally, if not spiritually, married. I decided an outdoor venue would be best, in case she needed to storm off in a huff. We got to Little Big Cup, a restaurant that resembles a strip mall in the front and a deck party in the back. I asked the waitress for a table on the terrace, hoping the calm of the bayou would help stem the inevitable rage. *Step one: get her in a good mood and make her smile.*

I pulled out her chair for her as she sat down. "So, have you been to D.C. in the past three months to visit your bestie?" I asked. That got a big smile. Okay, this might not be a catastrophe. I sat down across from her as she gave me the update.

"No, but she has been back to visit and to help with the Mardi Gras dances that her dance school does for the Krewes. Right now, she's gearing up for the Spring Recital. She's so happy; she says it's the best of both worlds. She gets to go to so many dance shows and is working in a dance school there while Etienne trains. Then she flies back here to teach her students. She's also helping the Louisiana University dance students, giving them classes to teach evaluating their progress. She's so damn happy. If I didn't love her, it would be really annoying."

Keep on this same track. "And, and how do you like living with Mawmaw Babineaux?" We paused while the hostess gave us our menus.

"I love it. I have never eaten so well in my entire life. My brothers do most of the hard work for us. I used to find them to be annoying, but they have been a godsend. What about you? What've you been doing for the past three months?"

Excellent, a perfect segue way to step two: get her to feel sorry for you. "Not, not much. Once the mission went south, I was in and out of surgeries for about a month. Then I, I spent the rest of the time doing physical and speech therapy. So, in a nutshell, pain, nothing, pain, and then a lot of work. Then, I, I came back here."

Renee leaned over the table. "Are you better now? I mean ... physically."

I shrugged. "Not 100%. The pain is manageable, but I still need PT and possibly one more surgery on my shoulder. I might even be able to save my career. We shall see. It more depends on the speech therapist."

"You want to go back? Even after all that?"

"It's what I do, Renny."

Her mouth curved. "You know I hate that nickname."

I grinned back at her. "Then, then, why are you smiling?"

"Fine, you can use it, but not around others. I don't want everyone calling me Renny." She scanned the bayou after that.

"My own private nickname. I like it." I followed her gaze and saw a heron dipping its head for food on the edge of the bayou. Renee exhaled, and tension drained from my shoulders, not all my tension.

The waitress came back and Renee asked, "Do you still serve breakfast? I really just want breakfast."

"For you, Ms. Renee, without a doubt. Do you remember MacKenzie Dylan?"

"Mack! Absolutely. Super smart kid! I remember one day he stole his dad, Coach Dylan's glasses. He came to school in them and said they were his. Meanwhile, his dad was searching for his glasses everywhere."

"Everyone thought he was just a bad kid. He kept getting in trouble and the other teachers kept wanting to put him in the behavioral disorder class. Then you insisted he was gifted. The bad kid, gifted."

Renee beamed. "He wasn't bad, just *canaille*."

"Well, now he's a Junior National Scholar. His first year of high school. He does summer programs at the Duke gifted program you suggested. He wants to be a medical physicist. I didn't even know what that was. Anyway, you get whatever you want, Ms. Renee. By the way, I'm Mack's Tante Di."

"Aww, thanks Di. I call those kinds of stories apples, and I just love getting apples. Thanks for that shiny, juicy apple. So, for you, I'm not a fallen woman?" she teased.

"Never. Besides, word on the street is you're not as single as we once thought. Just a soon to be mom." Di gave me a pointed look. "I'll get you the breakfast menu." Then she gave me another glare and left. Mawmaw Babineaux and her grapevine were messing with my strategy. Luckily, Renee was basking in the warm fuzzies of her apple story.

"I love when I can make a difference. That's my favorite thing. I hope I can get a job after Junior here is born." She thanked Di when she came back with the breakfast menu.

"Why, why wouldn't you be able to get a job? You're an amazing teacher and everyone knows it."

"Old fashioned hypocrisy?" She patted her belly. "I'm an unmarried mother."

"About that—" I started but was interrupted by Di.

"—Have you had a chance to look over the menu? Want to start with drinks?"

"Coffee for me," I said.

"I'm so jealous! I miss coffee." Renee pouted.

"How about some New Orleans roast pure chicory drink?" Di suggested. "Chicory is what they use in the New Orleans blends for the café au lait."

Renee brightened. "That's my usual coffee. They have it without coffee?"

"Sure do. My nanny has high blood pressure and can't have coffee. That's what she drinks and we always have some on hand for her."

"Yes, please." Renee smiled. "And can I ask you where you get it, because I want some to take home?"

"At *La Grocerie.* I'll send a bus boy out to get some and just add it to your bill." Di raised her eyes at me, and I just nodded. I had a feeling a delivery fee would also be added, a large 'you're a *tchu'* delivery fee. Once she had left, I tried again to move the conversation towards the topic at hand. I decided to explain how my actions solved all her problems. I figured that was the most rational way to go.

"Let's talk about your job prospects and insurance. Are those the things that are causing you the most stress right now?"

"So stressful, but I'll figure it out. My baby, my problems."

"Well, actually..."

"No, no, you helped me out, Armand. Remember, you did not want me conceiving with a 'rando' person, as you called them. I know you weren't looking to start a family or have a kid. This is all on me."

"It, it wasn't that. I just didn't think I would be around. I just had a bad feeling about the op from the beginning. I, I figured if I wanted to have a kid and I knew I wouldn't be around, you would be the absolute best person to take care of him or her."

"Aww. That's so sweet. I will take care of Junior. I just have some logistics to overcome." With that, she turned and scanned the bayou.

"Actually, you don't."

She hesitated and then turned toward me. "No, absolutely not. You're not going to ask me to marry you. This is my responsibility, and I'll take care of it."

"It's, it's our responsibility and actually—"

"Are y'all ready to order?" Di popped up next to the table with our drinks, at the worst time. I glanced up at her smirking face. She was doing it on purpose.

Renee pointed to the menu. "Yes, thanks. I'll have the crème brûlée French toast and the egg frittata."

Handing my menu to Di, I gave her my usual order. "I'll, I'll have the fried shrimp po'boy."

"First coffee and now shellfish. Are you trying to torture me? Next, you'll invite me out for sushi and a libation?"

"I'm, I'm sorry." Pulling the menu back, I frantically searched the menu for something else.

"Hah, you're too easy. I'm kidding. I will taste vicariously through you." Di left, chuckling, and I started again.

"The, the thing is, Renée, you don't need to be worried about health insurance because you have access to my health insurance."

Renee tilted her head to the side and squinted at me. "How? I mean, I guessed Junior would have access, but does the mother of your child also get health insurance? Is that a new military policy?"

"Ah, no. You, you have access," I took a deep breath, "because, because we're married. As, as my wife, you have access to full spousal benefits."

She scanned me silently from head to toe. "How bad was your brain injury?"

9

Brunch Blast

Renee

Oh no, it was worse than I thought. No wonder he waited to get in touch with us — he's having some sort of mental crisis.

"No really, Renee. We *are* legally married. Remember all the paperwork that I had you sign? My pre-deployment paperwork. Buried in those papers, with my will and power of attorney, I had our proxy marriage paperwork."

Shaking my head, because either he was crazy, or he was a dead man. I held up my finger. "I'm sorry, I must have misunderstood. Did you say that we're married? That we've been married the whole time you were gone?"

Armand nodded, and I closed my eyes to process that information. When I opened them, I reached into my water glass for some ice as my leg bounced in a nervous rage. Armand stuttered. "I, I, I just wanted to make sure if something happened to me that you would be taken care of."

I moved the ice from hand to hand, hoping the cold would cool my fury. "I feel like being married is something that I should be aware of."

"Well, it, it was in the paperwork. If you read the—" I winged a piece of ice at him.

"Dammit, Renee. It was just in case the worse happened." He wiped the water off his shirt and picked the ice up out of his lap.

"Well, you're fine now. Except I might kill you, but other than that, you're fine. Now, how do we do a quickie divorce?"

"I'm not divorcing you." The next piece of ice hit him in his throat and slid into the V of his polo. My aim is spot on. "Stop that. I'm trying to reason with you."

My lips pressed together as he untucked his shirt to shake out the ice cube. "I'm sorry. Who's being unreasonable here? The person playfully lobbing ice or the person forcing someone to marry against their will?"

"It wasn't against your will. God dammit, Renee." This time, I hit him hard in the throat.

"You do remember, before your 'donation,' how I talked about wanting to raise the child on my own?" I grabbed some more ice.

"Wait, wait. Listen, staying married to me solves your two biggest worries. You'll have my insurance and there's no way the school district will fire an Army wife."

I held my finger up, pointed at him. "You're not understanding me. You can't marry someone without their knowledge, Armand. It's just not done." This time, I just flung some water at him.

"It's done. You're married. You just need to get your Dependent Military ID card, and then you'll have a great doctor and some of the best OB-GYN services available in the state. No waiting for months at the free clinic — a doctor on call that you can talk to whenever you need. And, and free shopping at the PX at Fort Polk."

"Are you trying to seduce me with benefits?"

"Depends. Is it working?"

Di arrived, of course, with our meal. Curious about the by-play, she asked, "Do you need some more water? Maybe, just a glass filled with ice?" She was firmly on my side as she set our plates in front of us.

"Yes, please, with nice, big ice cubes. Di," I asked, "have you ever heard of secret marriages?"

"Of course, my great-aunt married a Creole man. It was illegal back then, so they kept it a secret."

My voice shook. "Have you heard of a secret marriage where one of the spouses doesn't know they're married?" I clarified.

"Do you want all of Meauxville to hate me, is that it?" Armand grumbled.

"What? Are you? No! But how?" Di asked, taking a seat at the table. Behind her, the restaurant got quiet. A lady at the next table handed me another glass of ice water.

"In case you need more, dear," she said, and winked at me.

"Sounds like everyone wants to know. Talk fast, Armand, because you have 30 seconds before I fling new ice at you and walk out that door." Indicating the front door with my chin, I folded my arms in front of me. Di leaned back in her chair, waiting as well.

"It was just like I told you. I wanted to make sure you were taken care of, but the Army has rules."

"Marrying someone against her wishes fits in those rules?" The question came out an octave higher than my normal voice. I took some deep breaths as Di patted my back and glared at Armand.

"I didn't see the harm. I really thought it would just be a happy surprise if something happened to me, and it felt good knowing that if nothing else, you and any child we brought into the world would be taken care of."

"Your dying would not be a happy surprise, you idiot!" Stupid pregnancy hormones. I started ugly crying.

"No, no stop. Don't cry. I'll do whatever you want, Renee. Tell me what to do, and I'll do it." He got up and attempted to hug me, but I just shrugged him off.

"You're so dead," I heard Di whisper. She was right. I had three hulking brothers, not to mention my parents, and Ms. Denise and Mr. Herman. And then there was his own mama.

"I'll, I'll make this right, Renee. How about this, why don't you just use my health insurance and I'll pay for the lawyer that you can use to take me to the cleaners? We'll just delay a little in getting a divorce."

"At least a year," Di offered helpfully. "You can't get a divorce when you're pregnant in Louisiana." I put my head in my hands and sobbed.

10

The List

Armand

U nsure what to do, I knew I was in trouble. *Think, Armand, think.*

I moved behind her and patted her back. "How about we go for a walk? We can discuss everything, and you can get some air."

Renee didn't lift her head, but she shook it. "I'm still on restricted activity. I'm not supposed to be moving around."

"A drive. Let's go for a drive. We can listen to some music and then stop somewhere to talk." Renee hiccoughed, but she nodded. I looked up at Di. "Can you pack the food to go?"

Di nodded and indicated the door with her chin. "Get her out of here, and I'll pack up your food and bring it to your car."

"And... my... chicory..." Renee said, trying to catch her breath.

Di touched her shoulder. "It already arrived, and I had it bagged."

I escorted Renee out of the restaurant and into my car. As soon as I had her situated, Di ran out with the food.

"Thanks, Di." I tucked the bags of food in the back seat.

Her mouth twisted wryly. "Don't mention it, but I will say you better fix this if you know what's good for you."

Shutting the back door, I hopped in the car. "Can you give me a half hour before you tell the world?"

"*I* can," she said, "but the rest of the patrons are already texting everyone they know."

"Shit."

"Language!" Di scolded.

"Merde."

Di shook her head. "That isn't any better. Get out of here and see if you can fix it."

I drove towards the Teche boat landing. It was mid-day, so the mosquitoes shouldn't be bad now.

"Ok, let's talk. What is going on? Why are you crying? What did I do wrong, and how can I fix it?" I zoomed down Highway 31 towards the boat landing.

"I'm pregnant, you! I have waves of rage and sorrow every day. Then you come with your pretend marriage. I'm going to be a divorcee. Men are going to wonder what's wrong with me. It has been so hard. People I thought were my friends have already turned against me. You do one little thing that's outside the norm and suddenly my friendly little town is full of minefields. "

Rage flashed through me, but I remained calm. "Which friends? Give me names and I'll take care of them."

"You can't bully people into liking me, Armand. Will you slow down? I'm getting motion sickness." She placed her hand on my forearm.

With an exhale, I eased up on the gas. "Maybe not, but I can teach some *mal élévé fils d'putain* [unmannered son of a bitch] some manners."

"That won't help. At least I learned who my true friends are, but Armand, it's been lonely. It's better with Mawmaw Babineaux — she loves me and takes care of me. My family is helpful and has never judged me, but Mawmaw is not doing well, and I won't be a burden to my family. I'm going to end up alone and divorced." She started sobbing again.

I parked my car in the boat loading parking lot and pulled Renee in for a hug. "You've been doing everything on your own, haven't you?" I said, kissing her temple. She nodded. "You don't have to do that anymore. I got you."

"I can do it. It's just the hormones. I'm fine." Using the sleeve of her chambray shirt, she wiped her eyes. I handed her a handkerchief as she pulled away.

"I haven't ever been a husband, Renny, but one thing I learned from Beau and Etienne is that if a woman says she's fine, that word doesn't mean what I think it means."

Renee snorted. "We're going to need to wash your shirt and mine. I should know better than to wear mascara. I'm just a mess of hormones these days."

"Not a problem." I reached over to my glove box and pulled out a pen and notebook. Handing them to Renee, I told her, "Write out your top ten worries. We start sharing the burden as of now."

Renee stared at me, pen and notebook in hand. "This doesn't mean we're staying married."

With a nod, I placed the items in her hands. "Understood, but let me help, Renny. I am and have always been your friend first." She inhaled and began to write. "Well, alright then." I grabbed brunch from the back seat to make a picnic while Renee worked on her list.

When she finished her list, she lifted her head. I'd already set out the food on a picnic blanket next to the landing. It was getting warmer, so I chose to place the blanket under a live oak tree. I helped her settle herself on the blanket and then held my hand out for the list. She hesitated, but eventually handed it over.

I started reading as she put the take-away dish of French toast and frittatas on her lap. At the top of Renee's list in her big

swirly script, she had the title, 'My list of my top ten worries.'
They were as follows:

1) Will I be a good mother?

2) Will the baby be healthy?

3) Will I survive the pregnancy?

4) If not (or if something happens to me), who will take care
of Junior?

5) Where will I go after Mawmaw Babineaux is gone?

6) How will I earn money and take care of Junior?

7) How will I pay for college?

8) Have I ruined my body?

9) Will anyone ever love me?

10) What have I done?

"Why don't you start eating," I suggested, "and I will see what
I can do about your list." As I reread the list, she started eating
her sweet cinnamony breakfast. Something about it reminded
me of her scent and ice cream. I shook it off, examined her list,
and took a bite of my po'boy.

"Okay, number two, three, and eight all have to do with
keeping you healthy and getting you back into shape. My health
care will take care of you and Junior. Also, I have a membership
at Blue's Fitness club. I can easily change to the family plan.
Plus, they have babysitting for when you need to work out, but
have Junior with you. See? Nearly one-third of the problems
have been solved. Also, four is easy. I will take care of Junior, if
something happens to you, plus there is my family, your family,
and the whole Krewe."

"What about the most important one? How can I know if
I'll be a good mother? Also, you need to eat more and faster so
I don't feel like a pig."

"I'll concentrate on eating once I go through this list." I took
a sip of coffee. "You being a good mother is the one I'm least
worried about. You have a great example in your parents; Mr.
Travis and Ms. Amelie are awesome. Plus, you have your aunt

and uncle. Ms. Denise would totally tell you to your face if you were mis-parenting. Mr. Herman would just nod and agree with her. I think I have a lot to learn from Mr. Herman."

The side of Renee's mouth quirked up. "You do. You're right, Tante Denise totally would let me know. Is mis-parenting a word?"

"As long as you understood what I said, and the word communicated information, then it's a legitimate word."

"Yes, that's totally what I want to avoid, mis-parenting," she said, as she sipped her chicory. She hummed her pleasure. "This stuff is good. Did Di add some to the order?"

Yes, for a hefty fee, I thought, but I said, "Yes, and if you like it, I will keep you in chicory, but let's continue with your list. So, we have taken care of issue one, two, three, four, and eight. That lifts half of your burden off your shoulders. I feel like five, six, and seven have more of a logistical feel. Basically, you want to make sure you have shelter and money to take care of Junior."

Her eyes narrowed. "Are you solving all my problems today?" She was making good progress with her meal, so I figured I was on the right track.

I shrugged. "Just putting them all in perspective. You'll be happier and healthier if you're not worried all the time. One of the worries that being married to me takes away is money."

Her fork hesitated. "How so? You're not rich."

"But I can get a VA home loan so we can look for our own house — a house in which you can raise Junior." With that, I took a big bite of my po'boy.

Her gaze lowered, along with her voice. "But what about when we divorce?"

"I'll put the house in your name, free and clear. So that is number—" I scanned her list. "—Five. For number six, making a living, being married to me means they have no grounds to fire you. Actually, I don't think they have any grounds now. I think you were just too overwhelmed to fight it, and they took advantage of that to get you out."

Flinching, she cut her French toast with vigor. "I don't want to go back. My principal is beyond useless. I did everything for that school, and they let me go without a thought."

I squeezed her shoulder and then rubbed it. "Then don't. You can be a stay-at-home mom. We won't be rich, but my salary should cover us, as long as we're frugal."

"But I love teaching!" Renee threw her hands up and tipped over her cup of chicory. Luckily, the lid was still on.

I grabbed up her cup, handed it to her, and gave her a peck on the cheek. "Just call Shell. You speak French, and she's been trying to get you to teach at her school for over two years."

"And do what with Junior?"

"Hah! You're kidding, right?" I chuckled. "Between my mom and your parents, for which this will also be their first grandchild, and their three newly minted uncles and our friends, the issue will be getting to hold our baby. Finding someone to take care of him or her, that's not gonna be an issue." Renee smiled as she finished her meal, took a final sip of chicory, and hid her yawn behind her hand. I patted my lap. "Relax a bit while we finish." Renee laid down, closing her eyes. I could clearly see the beginnings of a baby bump. "Can you feel Junior?"

Renee opened her eyes and saw me staring at her tummy. "Not yet." She closed her eyes, then yawned hugely. She was no longer upset. She had eaten something, and now she was resting. A warm wave of accomplishment washed over me.

I softened my voice. "Let's go through your other worries."

"Do we have to?" she asked. She closed her eyes again and took a deep breath.

"Quiet, I'm solving all your problems," I said.

She smiled softly. "Hardly."

Ignoring her, I continued. "I've solved one through six and number eight. Let's see about seven. College for Junior. You know, as an Army brat, he or she will be able to apply for the GI Bill and other benefits." I smiled down at her. With her eyes closed and her breathing rhythmic and steady, I thought she might be asleep. Thus, I kept my voice low. "So, number seven is solved. Which means I've solved 80% of your biggest problems. I'm pretty good at this." She was asleep now. With no fear of retaliation, I went on, "Aren't you glad I secretly married you?" She stayed asleep and must have gone deeper into sleep, starting to make this adorable snore, almost like a cat purring.

"And then," I whispered, "we have number nine: no one loves you, and number ten: what have you done? Number ten is easy. You've made a baby, and you're going to make a great human being." Her snores got a little louder. "It just takes a lot of energy. As for number nine, no one loves you. I have a feeling you're going to be way too easy to love." I brushed her blond hair out of her eyes and leaned back, enjoying the dappled sunlight coming through the live oak leaves as I watched the Bayou Teche flow by. "Way too easy to love."

11

The Babineaux Brothers

Renee

The sun was warm, magnolia blooms scented the air, and I felt comforted. My sleep had been poor lately, but for once I woke refreshed. My pillow seemed firmer than normal and there was a weight on my belly. My eyes fluttered open to the smiling face of Armand. His blue-black hair fell over his nearly black eyes. He was just so damned pretty. Thinking it was a dream, I reached up, caressed his face, and smiled up at him.

His hand cupped the back of my head. "Feeling better?"

"Hmm?" I tried to sit up, but he put his arm around me.

He leaned down and breathed into my ear. "Rest. I like having you here."

"You like ... uh." My face heated. I'd fallen asleep in his lap.

With a delicate sweep, he brushed my hair out of my face. "Do you feel rested?"

"Rested?" He smiled at my confusion or discomfort; I wasn't sure.

"Need some more rest?" As he said that, he brushed the hair out of my face. His fingers softly massaged my temple, and I went under again.

"Renee," something was nudging my shoulder. "Renee sweetie, we need to get up." My eyes fluttered open. I was outside, then it all came back to me, and I sat bolt upright.

"Relax." A large calming hand rubbed my back, and I turned to see his mouth curved with tenderness.

"I fell asleep."

"I know." He kept rubbing my back, making small circles.

"I haven't been sleeping well lately. I'm sorry." I pressed my palms to my eyes.

"Nothing to be sorry about." His smile widened. He stood up and offered me his hand to help me off the ground. I pressed my lips together but took his hand. After helping me up, he went to pick up the remains of the picnic. His movements were stiff and awkward.

"Did you hurt your leg?"

Armand rubbed his thigh. "It's just asleep. It, it went to sleep a while ago, but I didn't want to wake you."

My cheeks flushed again. I scanned the sky and the tree shade. Without a doubt, the sun was lower in the sky. "How long have I been asleep?" I asked.

"A few hours." He packed away the trash and leftovers.

Wincing, I rubbed my temples with my palms. Why couldn't I think? "A few hours? Why didn't you wake me up sooner?"

He kissed my temple. "You, you seemed like you needed some rest. You ready to head back?"

"Mawmaw Babineaux! She's probably worried sick about me!" I searched frantically for my purse.

"Relax," Armand said as he handed me my purse. "As as soon as you fell asleep, I called her. I let her know that you seemed tired and that I, I would wait for you to wake up before we headed back."

My brow furrowed. "But you woke me up."

"I could no longer feel my leg," Armand said. I covered my face with my hands. *I'm a hot mess.* "What?" he asked. "What's wrong?"

"Just please take me home," I snapped.

"It's not a problem, Renny. You, you were tired, and you slept."

"Home, please." I could feel my face blushing again.

He hesitated an instant and then kissed my cheek and said, "No problem. Let's go." He walked past, unlocked his driver side door, and packed the picnic basket in the back seat. I walked to the passenger side as he leaned over to unlock the door. The few deep breaths I took did nothing to help me. After my third fumbled attempt to buckle the seat belt, I gave up and put my head in my hands. I felt Armand's hands gently take the belt and buckle it. Then he started his Challenger and pulled out onto the road.

After a few miles, he murmured, "I, I like watching you sleep." I turned to him. He kept his eyes on the road. "It, it makes me feel, I don't know, warm, accomplished, like I've made you safe. I like it. I, I just wanted to let you know. In, in case you thought it was a hardship or that I didn't enjoy myself. Anytime you can't sleep, come see me, and I'll happily watch over you to help you sleep. I, I just wanted you to know."

My face heated, and I turned my gaze back to the road. "Good to know," was all I said. It felt like enough.

The trip back to Mawmaw Babineaux's farm, aka *Mes Rêves*, was quiet, but not uncomfortable. My stress and rage had diminished since the restaurant. As we turned onto the property, I spotted three additional cars there. Three cars I knew well.

"Oh, no!" I reached over and gripped Armand's forearm.

"What's wrong?"

"It's my brothers." In the distance, I pointed to the three men, their silhouettes clear against the backdrop of the setting sun. They weren't tall, but they were stocky, bulked up, and their stance screamed vengeance. Armand could take them, but there would be damage on both sides for sure, and I didn't want my brothers hurt. "Okay, here's the plan. I'm going to pretend to be asleep and you're going to gently carry me into the house. That way, they will rethink their plan to trounce you. Or at the very least, delay the plan."

"Or, or we could just talk to them." Then it registered with Armand that my brothers were armed with bats. He turned to me. "I, I could probably disarm them, even with my bum shoulder, but it would involve permanent maiming. Never mind. Let's go with your plan."

"Park out further, so you have time to pick me up before they get to you. Idiots."

While Armand agreed with my plan, he did not think that my brother were idiots. "My reaction would probably be the same if I had a sister." He stopped the car, and my brothers made their way towards me. Armand ran around to the other side and gently picked me up. I was very adept at playing possum.

"Armand Leger," Kevin called out.

Armand shushed him. "She's, she's tired and hasn't been sleeping well. Wait until I get her to bed." I really should have been an actress. I snuffled and then moved closer to him, snuggling my head into his shoulder. He leaned down and kissed my temple, and I smiled. Armand nodded to Jeb as he passed and made his way up the porch steps. Mawmaw Babineaux opened the door and as soon as we got in, she closed it in Eric's face as he tried to follow us in.

As we climbed the steps, I said, "You can put me down now."

"Shush ... you're supposed to be resting. I'll put you down when I get you to your room." Armand plopped me on my bed and raced downstairs. With no plans to stay in bed, I tiptoed behind him as he made his way back downstairs.

"*T'es pas bête* [You're not stupid]." Mawmaw said from the bottom of the staircase with a whiff of admiration.

"Renee's idea," he told her and she cackled as my brothers pounded on her door.

Mawmaw walked over to the door and called through the wooden door, "*Qui c'est ça?*"

"Mawmaw, you know it's us. Let us in," Eric called to her.

"Not my grandchildren. They would never plan to do violence on my property. You put those bats away and swear on your pawpaw's grave that you'll not hurt anyone, and then I'll let you in."

There was a pause as my brothers returned their bats to the cars and then assured her, "*C'est promis*, Mawmaw," so she let them in.

After watching them out the window, to make sure that they did not sneak in any weapons, Armand met them in Mawmaw's parlor. Since it was reserved for strangers' gradual admission into her house, she did not have any valuables or antiques in there that would be damaged if my brothers decided that her wrath was worth handing Armand a beat down.

"Explain," Kevin, the oldest, demanded. Then they all just leaned against three different walls, arms crossed, scowls etched on their faces.

"Did, did you know that your sister was saving up to pay for a sperm donor so that she could have a kid?" Judging by their faces, they had no idea. "I had a mission coming up, a bad one. When Renny told me she was planning on doing that, it just sort of came together. I, I didn't think I'd make it back. I really didn't."

"You were going to leave her all alone to take care of your kid?" Eric barked.

"That's why I had her sign paperwork. To, to make sure if something happened to me, if there was a kid, both she and the child would get benefits."

"What kind of paperwork?" Kevin, my oldest and sharpest brother and the lawyer, asked.

Armand hesitated. I could see he considered hedging, but figured the word was out, anyway. "Power of Attorney and civil marriage paperwork." Their mouths hung open as they exchanged bewildered glances.

"Renee didn't tell us she was married," Jeb said, tilting his head.

And here was the sticky part. I wished Armand well in explaining it, but his squirming felt like karma. "Well ... she, she didn't exactly know."

Eric snorted out a laugh. "You're dead meat." Then added, "Just because I laugh doesn't mean I'm not going to beat the—," he peered at the door, knowing the no cursing rule was in play at Mawmaw's, "—tar out of you."

"Fair enough, but can you wait until I get Renee calmed down? I, I know she's usually an imperturbable Valkyrie, but she hasn't been sleeping well, she can't keep her food down, and we need to keep her stress down and get her to rest." *Guilt. Nicely played, Armand.*

Kevin spoke for the rest of them, "Fair enough, but we reserve the right to beat you to a pulp, if you hurt our sister in any way."

"Understood."

I trotted carefully down the staircase. "Is everything okay down there?" I called down.

Armand moved quickly to help me down the stairs. "Everything is fine. Why aren't you resting?" He supported me with one hand behind my back and the other taking my free hand.

"I already took a nap and also," I blushed and whispered in his ear, "I'm hungry again."

"Of course you are, Renny. What are you hungry for?"

My response was immediate. I had been thinking about food for a while, as usual. "Now that I know you're all alive and uninjured, I can eat. I want Sweet Bourbon Barbecue pork from Poche's with creamy potato salad and coleslaw."

Taking my hunger as an excellent sign, Armand phoned Poche's for a plate lunch. While Armand was on the phone, my brothers all gave him their orders. Jeb volunteered to pick it up. Armand tried to give him some money. Jeb, being a *tête dure* Babineaux, rejected the cash. Armand let it slide.

I crossed the parlor and went to go sit in the recliner. Armand helped me to sit down and then pulled the lever to lift my feet up. Then he went to grab an old quilt from the couch and tucked it around me.

12

Negotiations

Armand

Once Renee was situated, she turned to her brothers. "So, except to try to beat up my baby daddy, y'all haven't visited in a while. What have y'all been up to?"

Eric glared at her. "I'm sorry. We've been outside, guarding you every day."

She pouted. "But you don't come in to visit."

"Don't *boudée*. You don't visit us either. Mama cooks Sunday dinner every week. We've been there, you have not."

Lowering her eyes, she muttered, "I haven't been feeling well."

"About that," Eric said. "Why are we just now hearing that you're not feeling well? A more pertinent question is why are we just now learning that you have a *husband*?" His slitted eyes emphasized that last word.

"You didn't hear about my husband because I just learned I had one today." Renee glared at me, but I just brought a straight-backed chair, set it next to her recliner and glared at her brothers. "You didn't hear about me not feeling well because I was busy trying to figure out what to do and I didn't have time to update you. I just got settled here."

"That's no excuse! We're your brothers." Kevin shouted.

I stood and growled, "You will not shout at my wife. What did I tell you about stress levels?"

"There will be no shouting in my house at all," Mawmaw Babineaux said as she walked into the parlor with a platter of her famous chocolate chip and pecan cookies and an old-fashioned white lacquered coffee pot. The scent of chocolate and coffee diffused the tension.

Everyone docilely replied, "Yes ma'am."

She held the filtered top steady and poured herself some coffee. The men all scrambled to help her into her seat. I wished I had grown up with a Mawmaw Babineaux. After she set everything down, she scanned the room. She nodded when she saw Renee was sitting with her feet up. She glared at my brothers and me.

"What we've got here is a failure to communicate." Renee snorted. Evidently Mawmaw adored Paul Newman, especially Cool Hand Luke. Mawmaw shushed Renee. "Hush you. You helped get us into this mess."

"Not alone," Jeb added helpfully.

"No, but at least Armand did the right thing." I nodded to her. Renee steamed. I could practically see her blood boiling.

"Without telling me." She grumbled and reached for a cookie.

Mawmaw's eyebrow raised. "And would you have let him do, if he would have asked?" Eric snorted while Kevin and Armand tried to stem their smiles.

"No, but..." I handed her a cookie, and she bit into it, because for Mawmaw she was defending the indefensible. She would have glared if her cookie hadn't been so damn tasty. Mawmaw Babineaux's magic cookies.

Mawmaw tsked. "No buts, you're having a baby. The man who gave you that baby needs to be involved."

Renee finished chewing and defended her stance. "Not always. There are nearly 11 million single-parent households in the U.S."

"Oh, so you want to be a statistic?" Mawmaw asked.

"No, I'm just saying it's done. All I want is a baby."

Mawmaw put her hands on her hips. "Really? That's all you want? Do you need me to get your wedding scrapbook? *La verité* [the truth], Renee Genevieve Babineaux."

"No, but that's what I was left with. I wanted a kid and nobody wanted me." Renee said and threw the blanket over her head because she was *honte* [embarrassed].

Mawmaw shooed everyone out of the room. I shook my head and refused to leave.

When everyone else had left the room, I leaned down to Renee's covered form and whispered, "I want you."

Pulling the cover off her head, Renee stared at me. "What did you say?"

I rested my head against hers on the recliner. "I said, I want you. You know that, Renee."

She stared at the ceiling. "You were just helping me out."

I snorted. "I was keeping you from doing something you would regret out of desperation, but also, I had no issues sleeping with you. I have and always will want you. You resemble Valkyrie from the old comic books I collect. Plus, you're smart and funny and ... well, I like you."

It was her turn to snort. "You want me because I looked like a comic book superhero?"

I turned and smiled against her ear and murmured, "She's a very hot superhero." *Idiot. What woman wants to be called a superhero?* I turned my head and pinched the bridge of my nose.

She stared at me, saying nothing, then nodded. "Alright then, we stay married until Junior here is born."

A quick 'no' jerked my head. "Absolutely not. We need to wait until at least a year after the birth. That's the most dangerous time for mothers."

She dipped her chin. "True. The U.S. does have the highest maternal death rate of any developed country."

Kevin called from the foyer. "Don't tell us that, Ren. We worry enough as it is."

I drew a lungful of air and rubbed her shoulder. "If I get shipped to some place with better maternal care, you'll be coming with me."

"I'm not going to die, Armand." Her hand instinctually covered her belly, rubbing protectively.

"Not on my watch, you won't. So, we stay together at least until you're out of the woods, and then I'll agree to whatever divorce and child support settlement you want. Deal?" I extended my hand to her.

"Deal." She shook it, and her brothers filed back into the room and sat on the couch.

I turned to them, and they all gave me clipped nods. "Excellent, one issue resolved. Now let's talk cohabitation."

Her jaw tightened, and she wagged her head. "No, sir. We're not sleeping together again."

Eric covered his ears and started singing 'It's a Grand Ole Flag.'

I gave her a cocky grin and waited for Eric to finish his rendition. "I can see where your focus is, but I meant me moving in here, permanently, or at least until you kick me to the curb. I need to be close by to help, and since you agreed we should stay married for a while, there's no scandal to us living together."

Crossing her arms over her chest, she countered my grin with the famous Babineaux *tête dure* frown. "I don't need help. I can handle it."

I softened. Instead of arguing, I pleaded, "I need to help. I need it, please, Renny!"

Mawmaw Babineaux came in at that moment. "Of course you'll stay with your wife." Apparently, that was all the privacy she was willing to allow us.

"Kevin, can you show Armand to the bedroom next to Renee's?" she asked.

Kevin stood up, shoving a tasty cookie into his mouth. "Yes, Mawmaw," he said with his mouth full.

"But that's your room, Mawmaw, and it's too close to me," Renee complained.

"Child, I can't climb the steps, and we both know I'm not getting better. Let me do. I'm old, and I want to arrange things. I'm so happy to know that you'll be taken care of when I'm gone. I'm going to try to hold out to meet my new great grandchild, but that's not up to me. Just, let me do, Renee."

Renee tipped her head, trying to hide the tears welling in her eyes. I placed my hanky into her line of sight. All the men in her life should probably start carrying a few hankies when they're around her. Her pregnancy hormones turned my Valkyrie weepy.

"Boys!" Mawmaw Babineaux called out, "Help your new brother-in-law move into my room upstairs." The brothers nodded and hopped to it.

I stemmed that order. "No help needed, Mawmaw. I just brought my duffle bag, and I already brought that over from when I thought I might stay with Beau and his family."

Mawmaw chuckled. "Lord, why would you stay there? It must be like living in a tornado."

I grinned. "It absolutely is, but I like it there. Having grown up as an only child, it's fun experiencing the energy in a big family. Plus, I like helping out with the kids; well, not changing diapers. That's not my favorite, but I will totally pull my weight in that stinky area."

"So you like big families? That's a very good sign, a good sign indeed." Mawmaw smiled and headed out the door.

"Mawmaw, it's only temporary." Renee called after her.

"Of course, dear, everything and everyone is temporary. No one lives forever. Now, everyone who doesn't live here, get out of my house. I mean to head to bed early, and I don't want any disturbances."

And that is how I moved in with Renee into her Mawmaw Babineaux's *Mes Rêves* farm.

13

BBQ

Renee

A dmitting you're wrong is never an easy thing. Not that I'm telling Armand. It's so nice having him here. He brought up my tea and toast, held my hair when I threw up, and then had a bottle of Perrier and some crackers for afterwards. Plus, he drove me around like a chauffeur. No really, he made me sit in the back because, statistically, it's a safer seat. When I argued, he called in Mawmaw to tie break, and she always sided with him. It was infuriating, sweet, but infuriating.

We were currently driving to my cousin Beau's house. His Krewe was cooking a huge barbecue, which was great because I was starving and I wanted barbecue with all the fixins.

"You okay back there?" Armand called back to me.

"Fine," I grumbled. I could see him smile in the rearview mirror.

"Is your mother coming?" I asked. It was a touchy topic for him. I rarely bring up his mom. I knew that she was what Mawmaw called a "free spirit." But I think Armand was ashamed of her.

"No," he told me stiffly.

This would be fun. Time to change the subject. "How is rehab going? You don't look like anything is wrong with you."

"I'm still only at 75% on my injured shoulder. The physical therapists believe I can get it back to 100%."

"That's good, and then what?"

"Then, I get to wait for the all clear from my speech therapist. After that, I go back to my job, and I get out of your hair."

"I like you in my hair," I said under my breath.

"What did you say?" I glanced at him in the rearview mirror. He totally heard me because he was grinning like a hyena.

"Nothing," I grunted, and turned to stare out the window. When we arrived, he helped me out of the car.

Pushing him away, I said, "I can get out of the car by myself. I'm not an invalid." I don't know why I suddenly want to punch him.

Shell and Gelly greeted me at the bottom of the porch steps. After they hugged me, Armand edged through, grabbed my hand, and tugged me up the steps.

"I don't need your help!" I pulled back my hand, but it threw me off balance. As I fell backwards, Armand grabbed my arms and levered me toward him. Swinging me up, he carried me Rhett Butler style to the porch swing. I frowned and crossed my arms.

"I would've been fine." He just gently kissed my cheek and then skipped down the stairs to the outdoor kitchen.

Shell and Gelly had both climbed the steps after us and were each sitting in a porch rocking chair with their lips firmly pressed together. I rolled my eyes at them.

"Fine, you have my permission to laugh." They rudely and gleefully chortled as they rocked back and forth.

"It seems to me you got everything that you wished for," Shell said.

Gelly stage whispered to her, "Hence the saying, be careful what you wish for."

"Can we please talk about something else, anything else? Also, I'm parched. Can someone get me some lemon—" Armand appeared at the front doorway with a glass of lemonade. He must have gone around through the side kitchen door. He put it on the side table beside the swing and then drew a metal straw from his pocket.

"Here, drink, you're thirsty." His strong hand held the tiny straw, and I remembered how they felt strong and warm on me — which really pissed me off.

"You don't know that."

He smiled. "I heard you ask for lemonade. Here's some lemonade. Stop snapping at me." With that, he whistled as he walked down the stairs. My eyes followed his jeans. God, he looked good in Levi's.

"Ugh!" I said, as I sipped my perfect lemonade, which tasted even better through the cool metal straw. *Damn him.* "He's so annoying."

Shell rocked in her chair. "Yes, a man who cares for you, takes care of you, and that you're also wildly attracted to. Must be—"

"—I don't know what you're talking about," I sniffed.

"Uh huh, how's that lemonade?" Gelly grinned.

"Delicious. Thank you. Subject change, please."

"Excellent, let's talk, baby. How was your first appointment with a real OB-GYN, and did Armand go with you?" Shell asked.

"How is that a change of subject?"

Shell's mouth twitched, the wretch. "Because the focus is on you and Junior."

"Could have sworn I heard you ask about Armand." I put the cool glass against my throat.

"Fine, but he is only a secondary character in this case," Shell admitted.

"Actually, he couldn't go, which he was upset about. He couldn't miss his reconditioning evaluation. He was doing his evaluation to move from Level I reconditioning to Level II. Also, it wasn't a real appointment. I didn't even get to listen to Junior's heartbeat. I just filled out paperwork once they saw I had insurance they would take, then they let me make an appointment. So, he didn't miss much, and Armand's evaluation was more important than him watching me fill out paperwork."

"Did he pass? His evaluation?" Gelly asked, "Because I can help with that. I have a class that I teach for the high school football players."

"He passed, at least this level." I sighed.

"Tell us how you really feel," Shell said.

"I know this is his job, but frankly, I'll miss him and worry a lot when he's away."

"You will worry no matter what. However, I think seeing him doing a tour de bras at my dance school in uniform — white t-shirt and black biking shorts — would cheer you up." I grinned at Gelly.

"I think you're right. Armand!" I called.

He lifted his head and bounded up the stairs to check on me. "You okay? You feeling hot or tired?"

"No, no. I just wanted to let you know that Gelly has a ballet class for the high school football team."

"And basketball — their vertical jumps have improved by over four inches!" Gelly bragged.

"And Gronk does ballet to keep himself in shape," Tanner added, walking across the porch with two beer bottles in his hands.

"Tanner Hebert Babineaux, what are you doing with beer? You're too young for that!" Shell scolded.

"Daddy asked me to get him and Etienne a beer. I even got to choose which ones." He beamed proudly as Shell glared across the yard with her hands on her hips.

"Beauregard Ulysse Babineaux!" Shell scolded.

"She three-named you boi. You're in trouble," Etienne singsonged.

"And who was the second beer for?" Gelly joined Shell in glaring.

"He did it!" Etienne pointed to Beau.

"*Couillons.*" Shell frowned at the men, took the beer bottles from Tanner, and brought them back into the house.

"Man!" Beau said and then trailed in after Shell. Tanner shrugged his shoulders and joined Etienne and Marc at the grill.

14

Bedtime 1.0

Armand

"As I was saying," Gelly said with a final glare toward Etienne, who blew her a kiss. "My sports ballet class is focused on strengthening joints and ensuring the flexibility you need. I have softball, football, and basketball players in the class. It would really help if you joined, then let your PT know why you're improving so much. I mean, you don't have to, but it would help my business, and I know I can help you to heal and recover faster."

I looked over at Renee, who was worrying her lip. "Was this your idea?"

"Yes, and no. I want you to heal, but I don't want you in harm's way."

I kissed her cheek. "I'll give it a shot. When's the class?"

"Wednesday nights at 5pm. Renee is meeting us all for lunch tomorrow. She can stop by the studio beforehand to give me your sizes, and I'll get you set up with the uniform."

I smirked. "So, I'll be in pink tights and a tutu?"

"I'd pay money to see that!" Kayleigh said from the footpath leading up to the porch. Marc frowned at her and she flashed her innocent, sweet eyes. She looked like a cross between Tinker Bell and Daisy Duke.

"What are you doing here?" Marc called from the grill.

"I was invited." Kayleigh rolled her eyes and straightened the bun on her head.

"By who?" Marc asked.

"By whom," Kayleigh corrected.

"Ugh, I'm surrounded by teachers." Marc shook his head and took a swig of his beer to hide his smile.

"I invited her," Shell said. "She has news, and I wanted us all to hear and," she glared at Marc, "she's a friend. So be nice."

"You don't have to be nice," Kayleigh told Marc. "Just polite."

"Ms. Kayleigh!" Bailey Marie and Sofia called to her and ran to give her a big hug.

"Hey diddle diddle," Kayleigh told them, and pointed to Bailey Marie to join in on the fun.

Bailey Marie smiled and added, "The cat and the fiddle." Then she pointed to Sofia.

"The cow jumped over the moon." Sofia pointed to Shell.

"The little dog laughed to see such a sport." Shell pointed to me.

"And the dish ran away with the spoon," Renee finished, chuckling.

I gave them my best 'y'all crazy' look.

Kayleigh shook her head. "Don't you read, Armand."

"Some."

"I do!" Sofia said. "Daddy read me that Best Nursery Rhymes when you were sick for three weeks. Remember when you came to the library with all those bruises?" The silence was deafening.

"Car accident." Kayleigh said. "My sister was hurt, but I'm ok."

Bailey Marie hugged her. "Your sister! Oh no! Is she better now?"

At first, Kayleigh didn't answer as she hugged her back. Marc raised his eyebrows; he noticed as well. "Not yet. She needs treatment. I'm researching now, but I'll find something. I just need some time."

Sofia hugged her then. "I always wanted a sister." She looked over at Marc.

"Not happening, Sof. You have honorary cousins, though." Sofia frowned at Marc, huffed, grabbed Bailey Marie's hand, and walked off.

Kayleigh smiled, but it didn't reach her eyes. "Anyway! I have some important updates to give y'all."

"Hold on," Shell interrupted. "First, let us enjoy our food. Once we get the Littles to bed, we can talk."

"I can totally help with that! Who's reading which story?" Kayleigh asked.

"Me too!" Renee added. "I call T'Alex, because I need to know what I've signed up for when Junior becomes a toddler."

"I can help with that as well," I said. "Logistics accomplished; now, *allons manger*!" We ate a meal of grilled burgers, fresh sausage, and kebabs of chicken and vegetables. We kept the subjects light. The only uncomfortable moment happened when Beau questioned Renee about taking seconds.

I pressed my lips together when the collective female wrath of the group was shoveled upon his head. Should have known better. I mean Shell took a healthy helping as well. They weren't just eating for themselves. *Couillon.*

After the meal, Shell, Beau, and Kayleigh read to the older kids. I scooped up T'Alex and carried him to the main bedroom to set him down in the new big boy bed. Renee was nowhere to be found when T'Alex let out a howl and had the most god-awful temper tantrum I'd ever seen. He refused to go to bed. I picked him back up and started swinging him in a circle. The tears stopped, and he giggled. Then, as I lowered my arms to set him down, he howled again. While swinging him around once more, Renee walked in.

"What are you doing? We're supposed to be getting him calmed down and ready for bed."

"Big talk from the woman who wasn't here for the mega-tantrum." I stopped spinning T'Alex, and he howled again.

"Put him down here." Renee laid on the tiny toddler bed, her calves hanging over the edge. When I put him down, T'Alex still cried but quietly and into Renee's shoulder. "*Pauvre bête* [poor little thing]." She motioned with her chin. "Get me three books from over on the bookshelf."

I got her three books, and she whispered to T'Alex. "Which book do you want us to read to you?"

Alex snuffled and looked up at her. Then he pointed to the *Where the Wild Things Are* book.

"Of course," I said, "because you're a wild thing." I tickled him on his tummy and he laughed, pulled the book out of Renee's hand, and situated myself for a read aloud. As Bailey Marie's parrain, I knew how to read a story, with different voices for different characters. When I finished, Alex was sleeping against Renee's side. We snuck out of his room, and she kissed me on the cheek.

"We can totally do this, Renny" I told her. She bit her lip, rolled her eyes, and walked away. Nearly an hour had passed. We clearly needed more practice.

15

Maybe DNA

Renee

While not a complete catastrophe, our efforts to put T'Alex to bed involved a lengthier process compared to getting the other four kids to sleep. How are we going to do this? *Compartmentalize, Renee, it's a problem for another day.* Tonight, we needed to focus on who is targeting the Littles and why.

We all gathered in the living room. To ensure the children didn't overhear, Marc positioned himself at the end of the hallway that led to their bedrooms. We wanted to insulate them from worry and create a sense of security. Once we had assured the Littles were asleep, everyone's attention focused on Kayleigh.

Kayleigh, normally self-assured and snarky, kept her gaze lowered as her knee bounced. Shell and I were on either side of Kayleigh, in case she needed moral support. I squeezed her ice-cold hand in mine and rubbed it to reassure her and warm it up.

"Okay, Kayleigh, you have the floor," I motioned to her while Shell patted her back.

Kayleigh sighed and lifted her gaze. "Long story short, I think it's my uncle. Remember how I told you I have an uncle, William Breaux? He seems to fit the criteria. He's rich, which the perpetrator would need to be if he wanted to buy the land L'Académie French Immersion school is on. He's heavily invested in gambling in Louisiana, which would have allowed him to blackmail Shell's ex and force him to give up the land for a casino. Finally, our family descends from the owners of Chretien plantation."

"You come from a crime family?" Marc asked.

Kayleigh narrowed her eyes at him. "No, but every family has their issues. Nonc Bill has always been a little pushy. He expects to get his way and when he doesn't, bad things happen."

"What kind of bad things?" Armand asked, moving behind me and putting his hands on my shoulders.

Kayleigh nervously pushed a blond curl behind her ear. "It used to be little things. He's escalated to things like losing your job, not getting a loan, stuff like that." Kayleigh was silent for a spell, then added, "He's gotten worse recently."

"Define worse." Etienne, ever the FBI agent, pulled out his ever present notepad from his shirt pocket.

"I was recently laid off of my EMT job, even though I have seniority over a number of other EMTs. My landlord has decided to evict me because after the job loss, I was a few days late on rent. Anyway, Nonc Bill said he would talk to my landlord if I would date his approved suitors. He didn't say it directly, but I think he thinks I'll marry whoever he selects. Like it's the 18th century and he could arrange a marriage for me. Anyway, I refused and about a month ago, one of the suitors was waiting for me behind the library one night when I finished work. Apparently, he had been granted permission to just take me."

"Take you, how?" Marc asked with a quiet and deadly firmness.

"He thought if I were compromised, that I would give in and marry him. As if." Kayleigh leaned to the side to make sure none of the children were near, and then whispered, "I escaped, but he got a few licks in. Before that, I considered all this might be Nonc Bill. After that, my blinders came off, and I focused on Nonc Bill."

Marc nodded. "That's why you didn't finish reading the Nursery Rhyme book? You were recovering from that attack?"

"No, after the attack, I had a car accident. I was in the hospital for a few days to check for internal injuries, and then I took a couple of weeks to let the bruises subside and to take care of my sister, who had really been hurt in the wreck. Let's just say it isn't paranoia if they're really out to get you."

Giving her a side hug, I asked, "Why didn't you tell me? I thought we were besties."

Kayleigh laid her head on my shoulder and sighed. "We are, but you were going through so much and I didn't want to add to your burden."

Shell squeezed her hand. "We'll work it out, Kayleigh. I promise, but right now, I need to know why he's after my babies. Do you know why he's after the Littles?"

Kayleigh frowned. "I looked through recent wills and public legal documents, and I don't see much. There was one document in which he agreed to the stipulations set forth in a will, but I can't find that will. I do know that Nonc Bill started acting strangely once his newest wife, Marlene, gave him a son, Brandon. He dotes on Brandon."

"So," Armand walked as he thought aloud, "how would the Littles be a threat to Brandon? How old is he?"

"Brandon is a 'three-nager' and a really awful one. He came to the library and completely emptied all the shelves in the children's section, leaving a colorful explosion of books scattered everywhere. He's a terror." She shuddered.

"The Littles are older. The attacks started around the time Brandon was born. Perhaps they're related?" With that, Beau moved next to Shell and squeezed her shoulder.

"Perhaps," Kayleigh paused, tapping her lip with her finger in contemplation. "Is there a father listed on their birth certificates?"

"No." Shell shook her head, looking up at Beau.

Beau added, "We didn't even need to get the father's permission when we adopted them. There was no father listed, and no father had claimed them."

Shell beamed up at him. "You claimed them."

Kayleigh reflected quietly. "If there's a will, an old one that's not available electronically, it might have something to do with family relations. Old Napoleonic law required that all children inherit from their father, both legitimate and illegitimate. This could be related to Brandon."

"It's a solid theory, Kayleigh. The solution is simple, then," I said, my mind racing. "We have someone with 25% of Mr. Breaux's DNA. We just need to see if the Littles DNA matches hers."

"Are you up for taking a DNA test to help the Littles?" Marc asked.

Kayleigh nodded. "Of course, I've already taken one and I'm signed up to receive updates if anyone I'm related to pops up. Actually, Nonc Bill is on there as well."

"Can we make sure he doesn't see anything?" I asked.

She rubbed her chin. "I'm not sure. You could opt into known relatives and then, for five minutes, opt into unknown relatives and then immediately opt out. There's a bit of a risk, but what are the chances he will see that? Unless he has set up his notifications to notify him of unknown relatives."

Armand set his jaw, his stance wide and unyielding. "At any rate, he seems to know something we don't. All we would be alerting him to is that we know what he already knows. I don't see the downside. Plus, the more we know, the better we can protect the Littles."

"What are we waiting for? Let's sign them up," I said. Shell nodded and ran to get her laptop.

On the way back to *Mes Rêves*, Armand didn't have much to say. Apparently, silence was one way to get me talking. I put my hand on his thigh. "What's up?"

He kept his eyes on the road. "What do you mean?"

I scanned him. Nothing appeared wrong, but I'd been friends with Armand for a long time. Something was up. "Why're you so quiet?"

"Do you think I'm chatty?" He bit his cheek. A tell I knew well. It was why I always beat him in cards.

My eyes focused out the front window. Armand wouldn't talk if he felt my gaze on him. "Not normally, but since you found out I'm pregnant, you've had a lot to say."

"We've had a lot to discuss and work out. Now we don't." Still, he kept his eyes on the road and didn't blink or twitch.

I forced my gaze to remain on the road. "Not buying it, Armand. Therefore, I reiterate, what's up?"

He might not relish a discussion, but there was no way out of it. He let out a long breath. "If you must know—"

"—I must." With my peripheral vision, I knew he glanced over at me. My eyes continued to focus on the horizon.

"You know how my mom is a bit of a free spirit?"

My mouth twitched, and I turned to him. "Yes, Ms. Rose is also brilliant, hardworking, and kind. She always helps us with school or library fundraisers and is a force to be reckoned with if you cross her."

He pressed his lips together. "My mama has a temper. Have you crossed her?"

"No, but an irate group of parents wanted to ban books from the library or burn them. They didn't care. She single-handedly funded a banned books section of the library. It's opt out for entry and parents can opt out for themselves and their children. Kayleigh says that's the most used section of the library. They have a separate fundraiser to buy books for that section of the library and that fundraiser brings in more money than any other. Your mama is awesome!"

Amusement flickered in his eyes. "That she is, and I know all about her. What I don't know about is my father or the sperm donor, as my mother calls him."

I guffawed at that, then I understood. "You want to take a DNA test, too."

"I don't see why not. I think it would be interesting to see if I have any other relatives out there. Perhaps I'll even find out who the sperm donor was. I also worry, since she hasn't said anything, if perhaps it wasn't a donation. If you get my drift."

I squeezed his tense shoulder. "That would be bad. Still, if your mama had you, it was because she wanted children. Otherwise, she wouldn't have had you or she would've given you up for adoption. You were undoubtedly wanted and loved by your mom."

"I know. I still want to know. I just don't want ..."

"To open a Pandora's box?" Moving my hand from his shoulder to his hair, I brushed his black curls behind his ear. I would miss those curls when he returned to duty.

He nodded, swallowing and still looking ahead. "Exactly. I also don't want to hurt my mom."

"Then let's talk to her."

"Together?" He briefly turned to face me.

Our eyes met. "Absolutely. We could tell her that with the new baby, we want a complete medical profile of all her relatives.

Then she can either tell you, or you get the DNA test. Or both, I think those tests are interesting."

He turned and focused on the road again. "Let's do the test first. Set it for private and then tell her. She could sell water to a drowning man and will undoubtedly try to talk me out of it."

I grinned. "She does have a gift for rhetoric." I pulled out my phone. "I'm ordering a test for you now. We'll set it for completely private and then, once we send it off, we'll speak with your mama. Sound good?"

"I don't know if I would define that plan as good, but it's the best plan we have. Yes, let's do that."

I finished typing and then stowed my phone. "Done."

"Well, okay then."

I squeezed his knee and then turned on the radio. "The Bosco Stomp! I love this song." We listened together, and I hoped it wasn't an omen. The singer sung about *les misères* [misery] caused when you love someone and then they turn their back to you. *Ça, ça m'fait du mal.* It will indeed hurt. A pain I was hoping to avoid.

16

Changes

Renee

The whole Krewe was getting together at *Mes Rêves* for a crawfish boil and to check out the Littles' and Kayleigh's DNA results. The smell of crab boil spices wafted through the air as I walked out onto the porch. Glancing over at Armand, I saw he was pacing the porch, stopping to watch his friends and then drinking his iced tea.

Armand hadn't told them he got tested as well because he didn't feel it was important. He did bring down his iPad, though, in case he decided to let them know what he had done. I was showing now. My bump was bigger than I thought it should be. Big enough that I needed rubber bands to attach my pant buttons when I wore pants. Mostly I stayed in sweatpants and oversized tees because everything was tight, and I was always uncomfortable.

"A truly elegant beauty," I snarked, as I examined myself in the mirror and squeezed my excessively pudgy bits.

"You ready up there?" Armand called up.

"Nearly." I tried to get myself into another pair of pants and I wasn't even close to fitting into them. I had never been a small woman. Hence the nickname Valkyrie, but blah! I sat on the side of the tub in my undies and t-shirt and sobbed. Did I mention the crying? My life consisted of tears twenty-four seven. I needed a new nickname. Valkyrie no longer described the oversensitive, bloated shadow of myself in the mirror. Whiney Woman, I grimaced before the dreaded tears made a reappearance. That's the ticket. Armand knocked on the door. Once he heard my sobs, he entered without waiting for a response.

"What's wrong?" He hurried towards me, his strong arms circling me.

"I'm fat and I cry all the time — like a timid little mouse." I pulled the scrunchie out of my hair and threw it at the evil mirror.

He rubbed my back, his large hand cupping my chin. "First of all, Renny, there is not a timid bone in your body. Also, you're not fat, you're pregnant."

"Why am I so big? I'm barely out of the first trimester. All the online pictures of pregnancy over the nine months say I should look the same, but with an adorable baby bump."

He turned me around, his chest warm against my back. Then he faced the mirror. His arms came around me and his hands rested on my stomach. "You do have an adorable baby bump."

"I'm huge. I don't want to talk about it. Can we just go?" I walked past him and halfway down the stairs before I realized I needed pants. "Ugh!" I went back up and he handed me my sweats. "This is your fault."

"We both decided to try for a baby, Renny."

"Yes, but you're huge. The baby is probably going to be like 15 pounds," I said as I put on my sweats, balanced by leaning up against him. On second thought, I turned to the closet and rifled through until I found one of Mawmaw's flowered muumuus, and threw it on.

He said nothing, but his eyes sparkled. Then, as he took my arm to help me down the steps, he said, "You're beautiful." I wheeled around on him, startled, and lost my balance. Luckily,

Armand was there. He just grabbed me up like I weighed nothing and walked me the rest of the way down the steps.

He kissed my cheek. "I'm thinking we might want to turn move your clothes into our parlor bedroom. I don't want any accidents on the stairs. I'll talk to Mawmaw to see if there's a check of drawers I can move there for you."

I didn't respond to him because I was in a daze and because he was probably right. Pretty soon, I wouldn't be able to even see my feet. Going downstairs like that seemed far from safe. He placed me at the base of the stairs, and I headed towards the kitchen — usually, a testosterone free zone when we are having events. I just needed a break. Armand followed me there.

Just to be difficult because I was in an undetermined mood and wanted to spread the joy, I said, "What you're saying is you think I'm clumsy."

Armand stumbled, "God, no. I wouldn't say that." We made it into the kitchen where Shell, Gelly, and Kayleigh were having hot beverages and some of Mawmaw's lemon cake. Now, we had an audience.

"What are you saying then, Armand?" I frowned, hands on my hips.

He laid on the charm. "I'm saying stairs are dangerous, *chérie*, and I want you and Junior safe."

A collective "Awww," sounded from the kitchen table. I rolled my eyes and glared at my pseudo-friends.

I moved to one of the stools at the kitchen island. When I wobbled climbing up, Armand's hand was immediately there to support me. Gah! It was so annoying when you try to pick a fight and the other person was annoyingly nice. "Fine, move my stuff down to the parlor, but Mawmaw put you in the room next to me so you could be on hand if I needed anything."

He shrugged. "Not a problem. I'll sleep on the couch."

With my elbows on the island, I rubbed my eyes with my palms. "Armand, you're too big for the couch. Have the Krewe bring two beds down."

Armand grinned. "Oh, what you're saying is you want to sleep in the same room as me? Why didn't you just say that?"

As my "friends" at the kitchen table snickered, I got down from my stool, grabbed a wet sponge from the sink, and lobbed it at Armand.

As it hit him in the chest, he said, "I'll leave with my win." Then he skedaddled out the door.

Gelly came over and handed me a cup of warm mint tea and escorted me to the table. Then she singsonged, "So, how's it going? How's married life?"

"Give me cake," was my response, and I took a vicious bite of the cake Kayleigh handed me and got back up on my stool.

Kayleigh scanned me. "How many months pregnant are you?"

"Great, even my friends think I'm fat." I devoured the cake and reached for another piece.

Kayleigh walked to the fridge, poured a glass of milk, and set it in front of me. I took a sip of the milk while she tapped her lips. "I don't think you're fat, but I was just wondering if twins run in your family." I lifted my head to meet her eyes.

"Her brothers, Jeb and Eric, are twins." Gelly told her.

"Really? They must be fraternal. They look nothing alike," Kayleigh said.

"Correct, also my daddy and Gelly's daddy, Mr. Herman, are twins," I added.

"Now, they look alike." Kayleigh nodded.

Shell set her cake down. "Your doctor didn't hear two heartbeats?"

Looking over at Shell, I tried not to be jealous of her adorable baby bump. She was further along than me and I was still twice her size. "All my doctor did was make sure my insurance would pay him and then he made an appointment for me."

Shell frowned at that. "You need a new doctor." She pulled out her Hello Kitty notebook, scribbled a note, and then tore it off and handed it to me. "This is mine, and I know she takes TRICARE insurance because I'm under Beau's. Have her give you an ultrasound first thing and check for twins."

I took a picture of the note and texted it to Armand.

> It's the contact for the doctor that Shell sees. Can we make an appointment?

He texted back immediately.

> Armand: I'm on it. I'll have you in for an appointment this week.

> Thanks.

> Armand: Anything for you, beautiful.

"Aww," Shell snuck a peek at my text from the other side of the island.

"Ugh, teachers and their uncanny ability to read upside down!" I rolled my eyes at her. "Enough about me and Junior. Where are we on the DNA results? Did yours come back, Kayleigh? Did the Littles?"

Kayleigh smiled. "I have cousins! Plus, since my dad and Uncle Bill were the only siblings on his side and my mom was an only child, that means the Littles are probably Uncle Bill's kids."

Shell grimaced and whispered, verifying that the kitchen door was shut, "It's very hard for me to think of the murdering psychopath as Pawpaw Breaux. He hired people to kill my babies' mama and Alex and he keeps coming at us."

With a tear for her first love, Alex, Gelly said, "The fire at the camp, the attack at the Babineaux farm, they were all to get the Littles. How could someone do that to their own children?"

Kayleigh pondered that while she sipped her lemonade. "Nonc Bill is myopic when he has a goal. He dotes on Brandon, his 'only child'. If the document he signed for the mystery will was an acceptance of a Napoleonic shared inheritance, that would be reason enough to get rid of the Littles."

"Ray talked about an inheritance. Perhaps from a long-lost relative?" Gelly added with a shiver, no doubt remembering Ray's attempt on her life. Shell gave her a side hug.

"I'll research that next," Kayleigh said. "But for now, I want to celebrate my new family and plan for Easter."

Mawmaw shuffled out to the porch from her nap. "Easter! You're having it here. You can all come over early and we'll dye eggs, and then the non-pregnant young people will go and hide them. I even have my silk egg dyeing materials."

"I always wanted to learn that!" Kayleigh said. "Did you hear, Mrs. Babineaux? I'm officially related to the Littles."

"More grandkids!" she said and embraced Kayleigh in a hug. Shell and I both started sobbing, and Gelly just laughed.

"Now let's do some serious porch-sitting and watch your men working," Mawmaw Babineaux said, directing us out of the kitchen and towards the porch.

"I don't have a man," Kayleigh said, her jaw firm. "And I don't want one. I'm a little busy right now."

"Doesn't mean you can't appreciate a handsome young man. The old married women get the seating area and the young pretty little thing gets the steps." Kayleigh smiled at that.

"I'm not old!" Gelly smirked. "But I, too, cast my vote for porch sitting, cake, lemonade, and eye candy."

$$\cdot\ 17\ \cdot$$

Family Crawfish Boil

Armand

Trying to rub out the migraine that was developing, I made my way to the crawfish pot they were setting up outside. Marc was purging the crawfish and Etienne was putting crab boil and potatoes in the boiling water along with something else.

"Are you putting in Brussels sprouts?" I asked him. Sniffing the spicy air, I hoped it would clear my sinuses and perhaps alleviate my headache.

"Prepare to be amazed. It was Gelly's idea. Her friends Luke and Sarah Hebert had a crawfish boil the other day and added Brussels sprouts." I grimaced. "Yep, that was exactly my reaction until I tasted it. Trust me!"

"I'll give it a try, but I'm suspicious. How can I help?" The Krewe of Roux was named after the essential ingredient in gumbo, because we loved cooking and food. Just then, a pain spiked in my head and my hand massaged my temple.

"Headache?" Beau asked as he was shucking and cutting corn cobs in two.

I nodded with as little movement as possible. "Can I ask you a question about pregnant women?"

"Sure, shoot," Beau said, focusing on his task.

"Did Shell cry a lot during her pregnancies?" The silence after that statement was eerie.

"What do you mean, cries a lot? Crying about what?" Beau hissed.

"Mostly, her body, her clothes are not fitting, and her appearance." Beau nodded and let out a breath.

"Socially based aesthetic construction of the pregnant body." Etienne poked the potatoes to see if they were cooked and added half of the corn.

"Nerd," Beau scoffed. "Also, it's too early for the corn."

"Explain." I asked Etienne.

"I only put half the corn in because some people like it well-cooked and others want it just parboiled," Etienne explained, sitting next to the cooler and grabbing a beer as we waited for the food to cook.

"No, not the corn. The social construction thing," I clarified.

Etienne leaned back and took on what I considered his professorial mode. "Women are constantly told what they should look like. Basically, tall, skinny, with big breasts. No matter what they look like, there is always a criticism and society is not kind to women about their appearance."

Beau reached over him, grabbed a beer for himself, and nodded. "Shell said something about that — that she hated her body until after her divorce."

"But the body changes are temporary in pregnancy." Armand said.

Beau did a face palm. "Do not tell her that! Tell me you did not tell her that! She's going to think you hate her body."

"Of course, I didn't. She's gorgeous. She has a bump." I smiled softly and made a gesture over my stomach.

"Shell is going through that now. Not just the bump, but with the emotions, too. It was worse with Alex. Now I know what to do." Beau scanned the porch to make sure that Shell was sitting. He nodded when he verified she was sitting and drinking lemonade. He went back to his task.

"Beau!" I shook his shoulder, annoyed. "What did you do to make it better?"

"I just showed her more affection. I let her know that I was still attracted to her body as it was."

"Beau, she's planning on divorcing me a year after the birth. She would probably wallop me if I tried to have sex with her."

Beau glared at me and turned to the others. "Did I say sex?"

"No, Beau, you did not." Etienne smirked the same way he used to when I would get in trouble in his Nanny Clothilde's classroom.

"What?" I growled.

"I said affection. Have you never had a girlfriend, Armand?" Beau asked.

Incensed, I griped, "I've had girlfriends—"

Etienne took a slug of his beer. "—Define girlfriend."

"A female that you take out to do things and sleep with."

"That's my definition," Marc quipped, checking the pot, and then grabbing his own brew.

"Idiot." We all turned to see Kayleigh a few steps away.

"I was sent over by the pregnant women to ask when the food would be ready. I didn't realize I was interrupting a testosterone idiot fest."

"Hey, now! Etienne and I were explaining the error of their ways to them. Also, we're adding shrimp for the pregnant women now. Less mercury than other fish or shellfish," Beau explained.

Kayleigh nodded and turned. "I'll be sure to include that in the report. I'll also tell them the crawfish and shrimp are going to be ready in—"

"—Five to eight minutes," Marc grunted, frowning.

"Well, at least you're good for something," she said as she made her way back to the porch.

"You boys are toast," Marc laughed.

"Enough, I still have no clue how to get Renny to stop crying. This is important."

"I massage Gelly's feet after dancing and her shoulders, as well — leading to nothing but a hot bath and bed."

"Nothing?" I asked.

"Nothing. You make it lead to something and they think you don't really want affection, that you're putting on the moves as a means to an end." Beau explained.

Marc dumped the crawfish into the boiling water. "That's what I'm doing."

"And that, right there, is why you're single and will stay that way until you change," Beau told him.

"I could get a wife like that," Marc snapped his fingers.

"One that you would want to raise Sofia?" Beau asked.

Marc made a sour face. "Hell no, any wife I could get like that I wouldn't want near Sofia."

"My point exactly." Beau said.

"So, affection will get her to stop crying?" I asked. "I'll do anything to get her to stop feeling sad."

"It will help, but remember, she's chock full of hormones. You'll have to deal with tears, no matter what." He took a sip of his beer.

"Super Bowl commercial tears I can handle; it's the sobbing that breaks my heart." I threw in the mushrooms because it was nearly time for everything else to come out of the pot.

We prepped newspaper on the outdoor picnic table and called everyone down as we prepared to eat. Once the Littles and Sofia were firmly ensconced at the kid table with Mawmaw, the rest of us adults could talk. We spread out the crawfish for everyone but handed small plates of boiled shrimp with tons of vegetables to Shell and Renee.

Renee started with the easy news. "Mawmaw wants the Easter celebrations here. We'll be heading over the Saturday before Easter to dye and hide eggs. Sunday will be potluck here with the whole family." We men just nodded and peeled our crawfish. No issues with that.

"Also," Kayleigh said, "I have an announcement. I'm officially part of the family ... well, the Little's family, anyway. According to our DNA, we're first cousins and because of my limited family tree, barring some illegitimate children, that means the Littles are my Uncle Bill's children."

We all stopped eating. Beau was incensed. "He tried to kill his own children?!"

"Shhhh!" I hushed him, checking to make sure the Littles and Sofia were not listening in. Mawmaw had them occupied with peeling crawfish for her and feeding Alex some mashed boiled potatoes.

Etienne, equally appalled, shook his head. "What kind of monster does that, and why?"

Kayleigh answered, "I don't know why. Based on what Crazy Ray said when he attacked Gelly, it has something to do with an inheritance. I'm checking into that in the public records; plus, at this point, it might be a good idea to engage a lawyer. Renee, isn't one of your brothers a lawyer?"

Renee nodded. "Kevin, I'll give him a call tomorrow."

I cleaned off my hands with sliced lemons and paper towels and quietly left the table. I nodded at Renee as I headed into the house for my iPad. I accessed the DNA site, quickly turned on the relative finder. I nodded at the results. Instead of making my profile private, I clicked to make it public, and went back outside.

"I think we have an issue." I explained to the table as I walked back from the house.

"What's that?" Kayleigh asked, wiping horseradish sauce off her chin.

I grinned down at her. "Well, cuz, you and the Littles weren't the only ones that took a DNA test."

"Cuz?" Marc stopped eating. "As in, you and Kayleigh are related?"

I smiled at Kayleigh. "First cousins."

Shell set down her shrimp and took a sip of water. "That means—" Her eyes darted to the kids' table, and she started to cry.

"Dammit, Armand!" Beau held his wife. Shell shook her head.

"You're their big brother," Shell said through her tears.

"Mama? You okay? Are those good tears or bad tears" Val called over, clearly used to Shell's frequent crying jags.

"Good tears, darling, very good tears." She looked to Beau. "Should we tell them now?"

"Yes," I said, "They will spread the word and maybe I can get the target off of them and on to me."

Renee started to protest, but I shook my head at her. We could discuss things later.

Beau called the Littles over to the adult table, "Guess what?"

"What!" Tanner said, thinking himself hilarious. I loved that kid.

Beau continued, "Remember those tests that we took where we asked you to spit?"

"Best test ever," Tanner said. "Easiest test, too."

"Yes, the spitting test. Well, we learned from that test that you have more family. Family right here at this table." Beau indicated the table with his arms.

"Really!" Bailey Marie bounced from foot to foot. "Who?" Beau nodded to Shell, and like an in-sync tag team, she continued.

"Kayleigh Breaux here is your cousin!" Val and Bailey Marie ran to hug her.

"But that's another girl!" Tanner complained.

Shell tilted her head and raised her teacher's eyebrow. "Tanner, that's mean. Go apologize to Ms. Kayleigh."

Tanner walked over to her, his gaze averted. "I'm sorry, Ms. Kayleigh. For a girl, you aren't half bad."

"Thank you?" Kayleigh told him and then she giggled and picked him up to swing him around. "So excited to have more family."

Beau smiled. "That's not all your family."

Val brightened. "Is Sofia our cousin as well?"

"That's another girl!" Tanner couldn't help but complain again.

"Tanner!" Shell scolded.

Beau ruffled Val's hair. "Sofia will always be your honorary cousin, but we actually found you a big brother."

This time, Tanner perked up. "I always wanted a big brother."

"Me too!" Bailey Marie agreed.

"But I'm the oldest," Val complained.

"There's just no winning." Renee smiled against my ear.

Beau told them, "Your big brother is Armand." Tanner and Bailey Marie whooped and ran to hug me. Val walked over and hugged me as well, reluctantly.

She kicked the dirt. "I guess you can tell me what to do. But it will be hard not to be in charge."

I lifted her chin. "I promise I'll only tell you what to do if your safety is at stake. You're still the big sister in charge."

"Promise?"

"I promise, sis." I lifted her high and hugged her tightly.

She grinned then and hugged me back, calling out to her siblings, "I'm still in charge."

Easter Prep

Renee

Everything was ready at the house. There were Easter baskets of treats prepared for each child, and the house looked like a pastel explosion. Shell and I, being teachers, had set up egg coloring stations with both the modern, regular dye and then one with Mawmaw and her silk dyeing method. We had also selected appropriate films to watch such as *It's the Easter Beagle, Charlie Brown*, *Here Comes Peter Cottontail*, and, of course, *The Bugs Bunny Easter Special*.

Our plan was set. Shell and I would relax and watch the movies with the kids while Kayleigh and Gelly covertly stashed the kid's decorated eggs around the yard, merging them with the plastic eggs they were currently hiding before the Littles arrived.

We each got a glass of refreshing lemonade and took a well-deserved break while we waited for Beau to arrive with the Littles. Mawmaw was taking a nap before they arrived and Armand worked outside doing yardwork and setting up some tents to make sure we had enough shade. We both sighed heavily when we sat in our recliners, putting our feet up.

Sipping on lemonade, Shell asked, "Did Armand get you into Dr. Daigle's office?"

With my eyes closed, I snickered. "Yes, and apparently Kayleigh was right. I get a two-fer."

"Twins! How is Armand handling that?" Before I could say a word, the front door swung open.

Armand barged in, calling to me. "Hey, if you're still up on your feet, you need to sit down. The doctor said only twenty minutes at a time and it has been twenty-five." Shell pressed her lips together.

"I'm already sitting with my feet up and some hydration." I responded. Armand peeked in the living room to verify, nodded, and left.

"Welcome to my world," I told her.

"*Pauvre bête*, Beau was a mess with my first pregnancy. He wanted to carry me places. Can you imagine? Poor Armand, it's not just his first pregnancy, but it's twins to boot."

Kayleigh and Gelly came up the porch steps laughing.

"They will never find that golden egg." Gelly sank into one of the rockers Armand had moved to the living room.

Shell's famous brow rose a fraction of an inch. "You don't want to make it too hard."

Kayleigh snorted. "We're pairing them up with their *parrains*. So, we needed to make it a little more challenging. We will have some easy one that Beau and Sofia can help T'Alex with, but the other kids are going to be paired with just their *parrains*. Etienne will help Val. Armand will help Bailey Marie, and Marc will work with Tanner."

"And," Gelly added. "We color coded the eggs. Pastel eggs are easy, primary-colored eggs are medium and the metallic eggs will be hard to find."

"I love color coding!" I sighed. "Now give me leftover chocolate." Kayleigh handed over some peanut butter and chocolate eggs. The scent alone made my stomach growl.

The corners of Kayleigh's mouth curved up as she turned her head toward Gelly. "Told you. Color-coding is like teacher cat nip."

Gelly just rolled her eyes. "Apparently chocolate is pregnant women's catnip." Shell and I looked over at that, chocolate around our mouths as our so-called friends cackled.

After our chocolate snack, we sat in the living room napping and rocking until Mawmaw Babineaux woke up. Once she woke, we went outside and prepared our individual Easter stations as Beau drove up with all the kids. The stations were a big hit, especially Mawmaw Babineaux's silk dyeing station. When it was time for the children to watch Easter movies, they all insisted that they keep their silk-dyed eggs and that Kayleigh and Gelly only hide the other eggs. They also wanted Mawmaw Babineaux to watch movies with them.

"Of course, I'll watch movies with y'all. Renee, grab the lemonade and cookies. The children will need some sustenance." I got up, but Armand rushed over.

"I'll get them for you, Mawmaw. Renee has been in the heat for over 30 minutes. It's time for her to lie down with her feet raised." I rolled my eyes, while Mawmaw Babineaux nodded.

"You take good care of her, Armand. I like that."

Despite the temptation to roll my eyes once more, I couldn't ignore the fatigue I felt. I let Armand lead me to our newly converted parlor/bedroom, where he left me to rest while he did Mawmaw's bidding.

19

Easter Surprise

Armand

I got Renee, the children, and Mawmaw all situated and headed back outside. The Krewe was all assembled outside. We planned some simple grilled food for after the Easter egg hunt. While we prepared the food, Gelly and Kayleigh hid the remaining dyed eggs and assembled some baskets for the egg hunt.

I'd been assigned to my goddaughter Bailey Marie. I couldn't wait to hear the latest updates about her life. I wondered if either or both of the twins would have a similar girly-girl personality like Miss Bailey Marie. Her unique way of describing the world entertained me to no end.

While we grilled and the Littles were engrossed in their movie, the sound of a truck peeling out from the back of the property caught our attention. Since the attack on the Babineaux farm last year, we all carried concealed. We vowed to never be caught off guard again.

We sprinted to the back, scanning our surroundings, but found nothing. We came back to the front to talk to Kayleigh and Gelly.

"Did you hide a lot of eggs behind the house?" Beau asked them.

Gelly shook her head. "Not really, just the harder ones. We wanted Mawmaw, Shell, and Renee to be able to enjoy the hunt from the porch."

"Let's tell them, no eggs are back there then. A truck just peeled out from the back and my spidey senses are tingling." I told them.

"No problem, cuz. We will let them know. I'm headed to get the kids. They should be finishing their movies by now. Why don't you wake Renee up?" Kayleigh asked. She'd taken to calling me cuz since our DNA match.

"Shouldn't we just let her sleep?" I asked.

Gelly snorted. "I want to be a fly on the wall when she finds out you made her miss the egg hunt. She will kill you dead."

I climbed the porch stairs. "Point taken. I'll wake her up, but from previous experience I will just say expect grumpy Valkyrie and not happy Valkyrie."

Gelly grinned. "You're waking her up the wrong way. Think Sleeping Beauty and not morning revelry call."

As they went off to prepare the Littles for their Easter egg hunt. I tiptoed into our makeshift downstairs bedroom. Renee snored softly, snuggled up to a pillow. Trying not to feel jealous of the pillow, I leaned down and gently kissed her lips.

My soft, gentle wake-up kiss quickly morphed into something hotter. Renee's arms came up and dragged me down on top of her. I braced instinctively, trying not to crush her, but she wanted me closer. She bit my bottom lip and then licked into my mouth and then we both got lost in the kiss.

We heard a clearing of the throat behind us and pulled apart. My forehead rested against her as I tried to clear my head, and I surreptitiously eased my hands out from under Renee's shirt. Turning around, I saw Mawmaw Babineaux, her hands on her hips.

"Renee Genevieve Babineaux, didn't you tell me that you were married in name only?" Mawmaw scowled but her eyes twinkled.

Renee winced. "*Oui* Mawmaw!"

"You have a funny way of showing that. Get up, *les petits* want their Easter baskets and since you helped make them, I figured you would want to watch."

Renee blushed. "On my way. Where are they opening them?" She darted up and then fell back down onto the bed.

Mawmaw Babineaux rolled her eyes. "You always needed some time to wake up. They're on the porch. Armand, why don't you go tell them we'll be right there?" She winked at me as I left.

It took Renee and Mawmaw about fifteen minutes to meet us on the porch.

"What did she tell you? Are you in trouble?" I asked.

Renee's head was swiveling back and forth and she was sniffing the air as she answered distractedly. "She said I should stay married to you because you were a hunk." I grinned at that, but Renee didn't seem to find it funny. She was sniffing like a hunting dog.

I stilled. "What is it?"

She took another deep sniff and then her eyes flashed opened. "Don't move. Don't anyone move. I smell snakes. Lots and lots of snakes."

Beau didn't hesitate. He herded the women and children into the house, ordering them to lock the door.

Marc rubbed his jaw. "Renee can smell snakes?"

"Ever since she was little and her little spaniel got bit by a water moccasin. I don't know how she does it, but she has yet to be wrong. If she smells a snake, there is a snake. Plus, she said snakes as in plural." Beau explained.

My head swiveled to the back. The truck, I knew something was hinky with that truck.

"Everyone, watch your step. I've called the sheriffs, and they're calling Animal Control. Fire if you have to, but remember, this is an attack by a human using snakes and the snakes aren't to blame." Etienne said.

"Shoot the snakes! Shoot 'em all," Renee yelled from inside the house. She was clearly not a fan of snakes.

Shell opened the door a smidge. "Just be safe!" she said and slammed the door shut.

From the backyard, we heard a bark and an ominous growl. We split off in pairs and headed to the back, watching carefully where we stepped. When we arrived, we saw a rough-ridden mongrel growling at a slew of *serpents Congo*. He took one water moccasin and shook it, yelping in pain when the snake bit him, but killing it quickly. Not stopping, he went on to the next one. At this point, the water moccasins sensed the danger and slithered away in a hurried frenzy. Gunfire awaited those who came near the house. Others were surveilled. They just needed to leave the property. Then they were Animal Control's problem.

The sheriff and Animal Control pulled up at the same time outside. We directed Animal Control to where the snakes had gone and then we showed Sheriff Trahan the large bag that stunk to high heaven. I smelled it now. Unmistakable aroma of the musk of snakes.

"So, it's not over," Sheriff Trahan said, holding the bag away from him in his gloved hand.

"Bradley, I told you it wasn't over." Etienne walked over to the patrol car and grabbed an evidence bag as the other deputies just gawked. He held it open as Sheriff Trahan placed the stinky sack in the evidence bag.

"You sure you don't want to come back to the Sheriff's office? I could use some help," Sheriff Trahan asked.

Etienne shook his head. "I'm pretty happy at the FBI, but I can lend a hand, Bradley, since someone is clearly still trying to kill the Littles."

Sheriff Trahan scanned the ground as he spoke. "Why do you think they were the target?"

"It's Easter, Bradley. What do children do at Easter time?"

Sheriff Trahan grinned. "Eat candy. My stepson Bobby always eats candy. I have to sneak it to him."

"Aside from candy, what do they do outside on the lawn?"

Finally, it dawned on Sheriff Trahan. "Easter egg hunt. That *fils d'putain* wanted the children to get bitten by snakes as they looked for Easter eggs. Oh, there is a special place in hell for this SOB."

"Sheriff, do we need to take in this dog as well?" The Animal Control worker asked.

I looked over at the dog, panting and lying on his side. "That's my new dog."

"Armand, that rangy mutt is your dog?" the sheriff scoffed.

I nodded, remembering how he did not hesitate to protect. "He is now."

"She," the worker said.

"She's my dog. I think she was bitten by the snakes. Can you take her to a vet? Tell them I'll pay for her medical expenses."

"Sure thing. It's your dime," the worker said. He muzzled the mutt and gently lifted her into the back of his SUV.

"Can you delay the egg hunt for a day?" Sheriff Trahan asked. "So we can make sure everything is safe. I have a pack of search and rescue dogs that I can call up to scare any lingering critters away."

"Not a problem," Beau told him, and went to let the rest of the family know.

Meanwhile, I had to explain to Mawmaw Babineaux how we would be getting a new dog.

After dealing with the snakes, we returned to find that the woman had continued with the celebrations. They had put on another Easter movie and while the Littles watched, our women hid plastic eggs around the house with candy, coins, and coupons in them.

Renee came up to me and shivered. "I hate snakes."

"Looks like you adapted to the situation." I hugged her.

She leaned on me briefly as the movie ended and then called the Littles over to explain the new hunt. The coupons offered exciting perks such as an extra thirty minutes of playtime, the ability to choose the family movie, a sleepover with a friend, and the highly sought-after exemption from chores for the entire week.

Tanner voiced what all the Littles thought. "What, we get an indoor and outdoor Easter egg hunt? Thank you snakes!"

Renee shivered again and sat on the couch by Mawmaw. "No more talk of snakes. Find your eggs. I'm just going to sit here with Mawmaw. When you're all done finding your eggs, come here and open them."

It took them less than an hour to find all the eggs. The older kids left the ones on the open carpet for T'Alex to find. When they finished, they opened the eggs and then exchanged coupons and candy according to their priorities. When the rest of the Krewe entered, the living room teemed with noise, excitement, and the sweet aroma of candy.

"Guess what, *parrain*?" Sofia asked. "We get to have two Easter egg hunts. We had one inside, and then later, when it's safe, we will have one outside."

I let out a breath and smiled slowly. "Yes, we will have the outside hunt later, when it's safer."

"Safety first. Safety always." Sofia said, mimicking her father, Marc's, security company motto.

"Indeed," Renee told her. "Now, give me some of your candy."

"It's not good for you or the baby," Sofia said, stuffing three chocolates in her mouth. "Saiffty firth. Saiffty awways" she repeated, but it was harder to understand with her mouth stuffed with yummy chocolates.

Renee turned to me, imploring with her eyes. "Chocolate!"

I reached into my back pocket and got out a dark chocolate bar with nuts. I broke her off a large piece.

"Fank you." Renee told me with her mouth filled with chocolate.

After having supper indoors, the Littles spent the evening constructing an enormous tent fort to spend the night in. Getting them to sleep was a challenge, due to the events of the day and their lingering sugar rush. In addition, Sheriff Bradley was kind enough to drop the dog back off.

"She's fine. A swollen paw, but they gave her antibiotics and a steroid shot. Where do you want her?" Sheriff Bradley asked.

"A puppy!" Sofia said, running towards the dog.

I put my hand on her shoulder to stop her. "A hurt puppy. Let's make a bed for her outside your tent. She's a guard dog. She kept y'all safe."

"Can she sleep with us in the tent?" Bailey Marie asked.

I shook my head. "She's hurt, and we don't yet know what she's like around children. Let's let her get used to the place first. Can you make a bed for her in the kitchen? We don't want her on the living room rug if she's not potty trained."

With a swift determination, the children dismantled the fort they had meticulously constructed, sacrificing the sheets and pillows to create a cozy nest for the puppy.

"What's her name?" Val asked, tilting her head back and forth.

"Cleoma," Mawmaw Babineaux said without missing a beat. Cleoma made her way to the make-shift bed, spun around a few times, and then settled down to sleep.

"Aw. Cleoma's tired." Renee moved her hand forward slowly. Cleoma put her head down and let Renee pet her. Renee put her finger to her lips to remind the Littles to be quiet.

"G'night Cleoma!" the children each whispered as they gave her a pat and made their way to the kids' bedroom we had set up for the Easter sleepover.

Once Shell, Beau, and Marc finished with their go-to-bed routines, the children finally fell asleep or pretended to. We headed to the living room. We had some planning to do.

$$\cdot \; 20 \; \cdot$$

Easter Research

Armand

"I had really hoped that Mr. Breaux had given up." Shell buried her fingers in her hair, ruining her fancy updo.

Kayleigh shook her head. "My uncle is not one to give up. If this is him."

"Since it was targeted directly at the Littles, I think we can safely say it was either him or another crazed man trying to get rid of an unwanted branch on his family tree."

Kayleigh assured us all. "I can guarantee you it was not him that directly left the snakes. He is deathly afraid of snakes."

"*Moi aussi,*" Renee said. "I nearly had a panic attack just smelling them."

Marc came in with a cooler of refreshing drinks, the condensation dripping down the sides. "I say we toast to Renee's nose — keeping us safe!" He passed out beers and cokes.

"To Renee's nose, and the pregnancy hormones that super charged it," Shell toasted.

We toasted and then and considered our options.

"Kayleigh, are you any closer to finding out why he might be doing this?" I asked.

"Actually, I have a request into the NOLA city hall for records relating to my family and any contracts or wills that might be related to me. They scanned a ton of documents and sent them to me on Friday via email. I printed them all and put them in my car. I was going to get to them on Monday, but perhaps we should all take a look," Kayleigh said, heading out to get the files from her car.

"I'll help you with that," Marc said.

"No need, I have them." Kayleigh raced out to her car with Marc hot on her heels.

When they returned, the teachers and librarian divvied up the tasks, handed us lists of elements to search for, especially related to inheritances or heirs. Marc sat beside me as we scanned our documents. He nudged me with his elbow and slid a note to me. "Is Kayleigh moving? Her car is filled to the rafters."

I turned to examine Kayleigh. Something was definitely going on with my newly found cousin. She had always been slight, a sort of tomboy Tinker Bell. However, now that I looked, she had lost weight. I made a mental note to try to remember to talk to Renee about her once we were alone.

Mawmaw said she was making us hot chocolate and herbal tea, then going to bed, "This is too much excitement for my little ticker," she said. Renee stood up to help.

"I got this," I told her and went to help Mawmaw Babineaux.

Mawmaw zigzagged around the kitchen getting everything together. She took a spoonful of the hot chocolate from the stove, blew on it, and held it up for me to taste. It was sweet and spicy. I moaned, and she smiled. "I had a Mexican exchange student come and stay with me. This is her recipe."

"I need that recipe," I told her.

"You stick with my granddaughter and I'll will it to you." She smirked and poured the hot chocolate into mugs while the tea steeped.

"That's what I want to do, but Renee deserves the best, and I'm hardly that." Thump. Mawmaw Babineaux whacked me on the back of my head.

"Then be the best. You will be having children together. You can't take care of them if you're out of their lives. Trust me. I know. I won't be around forever to tell you what you should do, but I'm telling you now. If you let that girl go, you're *couillon couillon*. [an idiotic idiot]. Now I'm going to bed. Send my Cleoma in to sleep next to me."

I sent in our new dog, Cleoma, that Mawmaw had claimed. She climbed on the foot of the bed and made herself comfortable. Then I left wondering how I could keep everyone safe and avoid being a *couillon couillon*.

$$\cdots \text{❦} \cdots$$

21

Easter Sunday

Renee

We woke on Easter morning and did our Easter egg hunt. Armed, the men each accompanied a child … in case we missed a snake. There were no issues though, and the children kept coming back to the porch to show me and Mawmaw Babineaux their treasured eggs. I had worked with Mawmaw to fix them some amazing baskets. We kept shooting secretive and excited looks at each other, knowing we had gotten each child exactly what they wanted, needed, and a perfect book.

After the hunt, we got the Littles all ready for church. We decided to repurpose my downstairs bedroom into an Easter dressing room so that I could be part of the process. Marc and Beau had gone to their houses to pick up the Easter dress clothes. Tanner stayed with the Krewe and they played video games while they waited on us. In the dressing room, Mawmaw had orange juice, coffee, and croissants prepared for us females. Since we were planning to have a big brunch at Little Big Cup after services, this was just a small snack to hold us over.

While I had my usual church clothes on, the girls had their fancy Easter digs. White hats, white patent leather Mary-Janes, frilly dresses, and matching purses. We oohed and aahed over their outfits, making them model them and then taking pictures of them. When we were all decked out and ready to go, Shell texted the Krewe to confirm they were ready to compliment the girls. They did such a good job with the compliments, except for Tanner, who couldn't hide his annoyance as he rolled his eyes and complained about the delay.

Mawmaw had surprised us by also dressing up, even though she no longer attended mass. She did her daily prayers and rosary with the TV in French every morning. However, she made sure that all the girls and even Tanner took a picture with her giving them their Easter baskets. They loved their gifts, and their books, and they each gave Mawmaw a big hug. It was adorable. I loved Mawmaw for taking them from a scary day to a perfect day.

"Y'all have fun today!" she told us as we were leaving.

"You sure you don't want to come with? We could come pick you up after mass to have brunch with us."

"I'm sure. Y'all have fun. Cleoma and I are going to relax together. You're gonna have a great day, and that makes me happy!"

"I love you, Mawmaw!" I said, suddenly and inexplicably emotional.

"Stop that! You know I love you too. Now shoo! I have things to do and you're in my way." I smiled and kissed her on the cheek, and we headed out.

After church, we headed to the restaurant for a tasty brunch of omelettes, smoked gouda grits, and everything bagels slathered with cream cheese. I texted Mawmaw pictures of the food, the kids, and my friends and family. She kept hearting each photo, a tech trick I'd taught her. The weather was cool; the food was amazing; it was the perfect day. I gave everyone a hug after brunch and Armand drove us back to the house.

He smiled down at me. My head was lying on his shoulder. "That was really ... nice."

"Nice is good?"

"Nice is perfect." I stretched up and kissed his cheek.

He kept his eyes on the road when he asked, "Can I stay?"

I tilted my head to the side. "You *are* staying."

He reached his hand over to hold mine and squeezed it. "I mean, would you consider letting me stay in your life?"

I smiled. "Armand, I'm having your children. You will always be in my life."

He pursed his lips and grinned. "Let me try this again. I mean, will you consider staying married to me?"

I didn't know what to say. I thought I knew what I wanted, but thinking of him leaving left me cold. "Let me think about it. The magic eight ball says, 'outlook is good.' For now, you stay, okay?"

He nodded and parked his Challenger. He rounded the hood and opened the door for me. "I'll take that as a definite, maybe." He leaned down and kissed my cheek.

The curtains in an upstairs room fluttered. "I think we have an audience." Then I straightened. Mawmaw shouldn't be upstairs. Under no circumstances should she be climbing stairs with her heart condition.

"Something's wrong!" I ran to the house, but Armand stopped me before I could enter and made me wait on the porch.

"It looks undisturbed. I don't see anything out of place. Mawmaw!" He called.

My phone dinged. Mawmaw texted me.

> MawmawB: I'm upstairs.

I walked in the door. "She just texted, Armand. She's upstairs." I scanned the downstairs. Armand wasn't wrong. Nothing was disturbed. In fact, everything was immaculately clean, without a single speck of dust in sight. "Oh no, oh no!" I ran upstairs.

Armand caught up with me and picked me up. "Which room?"

"The one you stayed in when we were upstairs."

He brought me there and deposited me next to Mawmaw's bed.

"Hello *ma chèrie*, did you have a good day?" She was cuddled up with Cleoma, petting her as she lay back.

Tears welled in my eyes, but I kept my voice calm. "It was a perfect day."

"That's what I thought as well. A perfect day." She patted my hand.

"Mawmaw, why did you clean the house? That must have been hard for you?"

"Not at all. I had a burst of energy. Besides, your pawpaw was always a stickler for a clean house. I wanted to make sure it was nice and neat for him."

"You can't go." I vehemently shook my head.

"I can and I will. I'm old and tired and you said yourself, it's the perfect day."

I cried. "It won't be perfect without you. Plus, you won't meet your twin grandchildren."

"I have met them, and you will be naming one of them after me. Plus, now I know you have someone looking out for you." She focused on Armand, who nodded to her. She nodded back. "I won't worry so much. Now let me sleep, child."

I laid my head on her shoulder. "Tell Pawpaw I love him."

"He knows." She drew her fingers through my hair. "He says you got my hair. He always loved my hair."

"I don't know what to do. Should I call everyone?" I murmured.

"No, dear, no need to make a fuss. It won't be a surprise. Besides, I will make it through the day. I don't plan to ruin your perfect day," she said. "Armand, take those envelopes. I trust you to take care of what is in them." He reached down and grabbed them up.

"What should I do? I don't know what to do, Mawmaw." Tears streamed down my cheeks.

"Just hold my hand, dear. Can you do that? Here, come to bed, so you're comfortable." She scooted over and I laid next to her.

Taking her hand, I pulled out my phone and pulled up *Le Petit Prince*. It had always been one of our favorite stories. I read it to her until she fell asleep. Armand placed the chair beside me. When I finished reading, he held my other hand. With a huge yawn, I too fell asleep.

When I woke up the next morning, she was gone. I went to her dresser and sniffed her Shalimar perfume. Pawpaw would buy it for her for each anniversary. I closed my eyes and remembered. The babies kicked. "You miss her, too," I told them. Then, I called for Armand.

22

Au Revoir

Armand

I woke up to sobbing, and Renee calling my name. The most god-awful sound you ever heard. Renee had moved off the bed and was holding Mawmaw's hand. I texted Ms. Denise and Ms. Amelie so she could break the news to Mr. Herman and the rest of the family. The rest of the day, I just stayed near Renee. She was heartbroken. I was worried about her and I was worried about the twins. The house buzzed with the constant ebb and flow of family and friends, coming in and out to lend a hand. Father LeBrun arrived mid-morning.

He enfolded Renee in a hug. Well, he tried anyway, but he was a 5'8" Creole man and she was a six foot Viking.

She sobbed. "We didn't get to give her last rites!"

He patted her mid-back. "She took care of that last week. She knew what was coming, but she wanted one more Easter with the family. Was it a good one?"

Renee nodded. "Well, apart from the snakes, it was probably one of the best we've ever had."

He pulled away. "Snakes?"

I grabbed Armand's hand once I pulled away from Father LeBrun. His lip quirked up. "Long story. Let's just say, a bad person left them, and Armand and his Krewe scared them away, along with Cleoma, who we will need you to bless."

"Not a problem. Armand chased away the snakes?" Father Lebrun pressed his lips together.

"Yes."

With teasing laughter in his eyes, he said, "Armand Patrick Leger. Chased all the snakes away."

Renee's reaction was a mix of laughter and tears. "I guess his saint's name is apt. Like St. Patrick, he got rid of the snakes."

Father, Renee, and I worked together to plan for Mawmaw's services. She had actually left a plan with him that we followed to a T. The papers that she had handed me even included the menu we needed to cater from Myran's House of Manger. Mawmaw served us all sweet, cool milkshakes, crunchy onion rings, and salty French fries. They already had her order and Myran's even delivered it to us. We had the wake at the funeral home the next day, and then she was buried next to her husband, Pawpaw Babineaux.

Renee smiled sadly as she was lowered into the ground. "Just like she always wanted to be."

The day after the funeral, the call from Hercule Trahan Esquire came. He was our family lawyer and had helped Mawmaw write her will. He told us that both Renee and I were listed as beneficiaries.

We met in the conference room of Mr. Trahan's office. Mawmaw Babineaux's baby brother, Nonc Pervis, was trying to comfort his nieces and nephews, as well as his grandnieces and nephews. Renee snuck into the room amongst all the hullabaloo and sat in the corner. I moved a chair over, got her a glass of water from the pitcher on the table, and waited with her.

Mr. Trahan began, "I know you're all good friends and family to Mrs. Aida Babineaux. Please accept my deepest condolences. As she was kind and generous in life, so she has been in her death. She was also a little *canaille*. As you know, she lived on and off her farm. She and David lived off social security and pensions, but they also had some investments made each time they sold off cattle or land. In short, Mrs. Babineaux was a wealthy woman…"

It all sort of blurred after that. What I did remember is that she left Renee 90% of the farm and me the other 10%. "To encourage you to stay together," Mr. Trahan said.

She also left Renee money for upkeep and to make sure she could stay home with the twins for the first three years of their lives. Then she said she strongly encouraged us to enroll them at L'Académie Immersion school. She wanted all her great grandchildren to speak French.

After the reading of the will, Renee turned to me and asked, "What do we do now?"

"Go home." I told her. Tears welled in her eyes as she nodded.

Upon our return, the house seemed different because it was now ours and because it felt so empty.

Over the next weeks, Renee went on a cleaning jag. In addition, she invited Mawmaw's other grandchildren, her brothers, and cousins, Beau and Gelly, to come and choose anything they wanted. Filling the house with Mawmaw's family seemed, right. Together, we cleaned and decluttered the house. Gelly and Renee split Mawmaw's jewelry, except for the rings. Her brothers and Beau took the rings. Beau gave his to Shell, and Renee's brothers kept theirs in case they changed their bachelor ways.

"Not that we expect to change our ways, but never say never," Kevin said, pocketing his ring. I noticed Renee looked at the rings with longing and then search the remaining jewelry.

Mawmaw had slipped me Renny's favorite ring — an elegant emerald and sapphire ring with filigree, set in white gold, a week before she passed.

Renee glanced up from her search to roll her eyes at her older brother. "Of course not."

We spent the day telling stories about Mawmaw and remembering her. At my request, Renee's brothers and Beau took most of Mawmaw's ceramic figurines. I was walking into the living room when I heard her ask about them.

"Why would you want those?" she asked Eric as he rolled his in newspaper.

He averted his gaze and said, "Less for you to dust." His brothers laughed like loons.

"What's going on, Jeb?" Renee asked, focusing on Jeb, the dratted weak link who was terrible at lying.

Jeb raised his hands in surrender. "It was a special request from Armand. Apparently, you used Mawmaw's precious ceramics as projectiles."

"Armand!" Renee yelled.

"Oui, chérie?" I said from behind her.

Her cowardly brothers fled the scene, taking the ceramics with them. Renee gave me sweet eyes and a butter-would-not-melt smile as she walked toward the sofa.

"Did you ask my cousin and my brothers to take all of Mawmaw's ceramic figurines?" She grabbed up a sofa pillow and began fluffing it.

I scratched my head. "Umm, well, I didn't want you to feel guilty or bad if you broke one of her heirloom pieces. Plus, they require a lot of dusting."

She tilted her head, and her lips quirked up. "So, it wasn't self-preservation?"

I hesitated, but couldn't lie. "Those damn figurines hurt when you throw them."

She launched all four sofa pillows at me in quick succession.

"Dammit, Renee!" I said as three of the four hit me in the face. "You're just making my point."

"And I'm underlining that getting rid of the ceramics won't keep me from keeping you in line in a manner that I see fit." I rushed her, then pulled her gently into my arms as I fell back on the sofa. She landed on top of me, and I let out a 'humph.'

"I can think of better ways to keep me in line." I pulled her head down, wrapped a leg around her, and delved into her mouth.

I was surfing on that sensation when I heard, "Ugh Renee! Not while we're here!" I lifted my head, and Eric was covering his eyes.

"Maybe it's time for you to leave," Renee told him.

"We were just leaving," Shell tittered from behind the door. She grabbed Eric's arm and then, after a flurry of 'goodbyes,' we were alone. After a stellar make-out session and a brief siesta for Renee, we strolled through the garden.

"We should make a homestead," Renee said as we walked through the rows of vegetables.

23

Homestead

Renee

"A homestead?" Armand said, picking the broccoli, cabbage, and greens and putting them in his basket.

"Yes, a self-sustainable home," I said, scanning the property. "You have gardens for food. What else do you need?"

Pointing to different sections where I envisioned different elements, I elaborated. "A well for water, some solar panels, and a generator for energy. Some chickens for eggs. Some goats for milk and lawn maintenance. Some horses to ride."

Armand laughed. "We need horses to have a homestead?"

I winked at him. "No, I just want some horses to ride."

"I tell you what, you get a cosplay Valkyrie outfit and ride a horse in it, and I promise to get horses for our homestead."

"Careful what you wish for." I glanced down at my stomach. "Fine, I can't do it now, but just you wait."

"I look forward to the show. Let's make a list of every home-steady thing you want to do." Armand helped me onto the porch and let me rattle off ideas until I was tired. Then he brought me inside for some iced tea before I laid down for a nap. It had been an exhausting time.

I woke the next day to noises emanating from my front porch. My brothers, my cousin Beau, his friend Marc and the all the Littles were all there (we had expanded them to encompass all the little kids in our circle — I couldn't wait until our children joined their ranks).

"Uh ... what's going on?"

Shell turned around, holding young Alex in her arms, and smiled at me. "What's going on is I organized them into groups and assigned them tasks. We'll be doing our badge training over here so that you can set up your homestead."

Valerie smiled up at her, adorable in a big white floppy hat. "We've been planning all the gardens for the Habitat homes and now we get to plan your garden expansion."

Bailey Marie chimed in, "I'm creating a cut flower garden around the house."

"And I'm planting the fruit orchard," Sofia boasted. All three girls wore Little House on the Prairie bonnets that they hand sewed themselves.

"I'll do your *potager* and herb garden. You just need to let me know which veggies and which herbs you want planted," Kayleigh said.

Beau chimed in as well. "Armand and I will be creating your chicken coop and a pen for your goats. We'll have a path from the house, but we're keeping it away from the house and added some guinea chickens because they kill snakes."

"At the mention of the 'S' word, I will just say that you'll be gathering the eggs from the chickens," I told Armand.

Armand pointed to Marc, who was walking up with several men. "Marc and his crew will be setting up the security system."

I frowned. "Is a security system part of a homestead? I've never seen that on *Homestead Rescue*."

"It's in yours. You've already been targeted once. If I get called away, I need to know that you're safe," Armand said.

I frowned at the mention of Armand leaving. He seemed to take it as a good sign. He leaned over and planted a gentle kiss on my lips.

The Krewe and the Littles worked all day. By the end of the day, my dream of a homestead was nearly complete. With a glass of cold ginger ale in one hand and a handful of cheesy crackers in the other, I settled onto the porch. Armand worked on the goat pen's last slats. I, in no way, stared at his hands, his forearms, or his well-formed backside. That would be gauche.

"You know, we could put livestock to slaughter in here. We probably need more protein," he said.

I scrunched up my face. "Sounds bloody and violent. Let's change it to a calm pond."

"Can we stock it with fish?" He climbed the porch stairs and sat next to me on the porch swing.

I held out my hand. "Deal. As long as I never have to scale or filet the fish."

Armand shook my hand to seal the deal and then leaned back and swung. "Saturdays fishing with the twins. That sounds fun."

During the next week, Marc came out to set up our security system. Armed with measuring tools, Beau evaluated the greenhouse's sun exposure, taking note of every angle and shadow. Finally, at the end of the week, Armand brought over a collection of fluffy chirping chicks. Cleoma sniffed them with interest.

"They're so cute!" I turned to Cleoma. "Not for you!" She whined but took it philosophically.

Armand set the last chick free in the coop. "Yes, and those guinea ones are going to be noisy."

Marc walked up. "Those chicks and Cleoma are your old school defense. If someone disables the security system, they'll still warn you of danger."

"So, Plan B?" I asked.

He nodded. "Let me show you Plan A." He directed me to the house.

"Sit here," he pointed to the porch swing, and I sat. Armand sat next to me.

"First level of protection. An indicator that someone has breached your perimeter."

I chuckled and whispered in Armand's ear, "That sounds … dirty."

He closed his eyes and then said, "Pay attention, Renee. I need you all safe."

I sniffed. "Fine, go on."

Marc demonstrated the app on the phone, which indicated when anything crossed into our land. Plus, the gate and door ringers allowed us to control who entered the property. He had panic buttons for my phone, keys, and in each room. In addition, there were fire and CO_2 detectors on both floors.

"Finally," he said and walked me to my Mawmaw's old room off the kitchen. Inside, Armand had moved all my things. He also had a daybed in there so he could sleep. Marc crossed the room and opened the closet door. "Look in here."

"Narnia?" I asked, and he smiled because that was one of Sofia's favorite stories.

"Not quite, but a safe haven for sure."

Upon entering, I noticed a sturdy metal door blocking my way. I squinted. "You built a metal room into my closet?"

Marc rubbed his hands together. "It's a modular safe room, with off-grid power via solar on the roof with battery powered backup."

Armand took over like a kid in a candy store. "It's fireproof, hurricane proof and can withstand a tornado up to 250 miles per hour. Look! It has two-fold down bunks and includes a three-month food survival kit and three months of water for up to four people and a complete first aid kit." Beau walked in then. "It even has a latrine."

"You mean a bathroom?"

"It's more of a composting toilet," Armand corrected.

My gaze swept across the panic room, taking in their child-like glee, before a chuckle escaped my lips. "You're all closet preppers!"

None of them answered. "Marc, do you have a panic room in your house along with a three-month stash of supplies?"

"Of course, but I'm a security professional. I had mine built into the house when I had it constructed. Plus, I can make Sofia's room into a safe room at the push of a button."

"Do you have a panic room and supplies, Beau?"

"Not a panic room per se, just an interior room. The cost of the build was too expensive for Shell to let me build that. That's why I wanted to see the modular structure. It's less expensive to build."

"So, when I told Armand that I wanted to homestead, did y'all just see it as a way to test out some of your ideas before you do them at home?"

I heard crickets, and then Armand distracted me. "So where do you want us to dig you a pond?"

As long as I was getting my way, I directed, "Southwest quadrant and I want a dock and a canoe as well."

Armand kissed my temple. "We're on it. Stay here and take a moment to enjoy your safe room. Explore. There are some surprises you will appreciate."

Armand pulled down the bunk from the wall, and I sat down on it. They walked out, leaving me in solitude as the door closed behind them. As they left, I noticed a sliding compartment next to the bunk. Inside there were my favorite romance novel writers' best series. I recognized Kayleigh's hand in this as well. I laid in my bunk and pulled out my favorite novel, *To Sir Philip with Love* by Julia Quinn. After reading for an hour, fatigue overtook me and I fell asleep feeling safe and sound. Not that I would admit to Armand that he was right — sets a bad precedent.

Later, I was working with the Littles planting seeds in our new green house, when a cramp took me. I rolled into a fetal position. Tanner screamed and ran for help.

Within a few minutes, Armand arrived. "Ambulance is on its way. They said to stay still and I need to keep you comfortable."

"I can't lose these babies, Armand. These are the babies that Mawmaw spoke with. They're our first and second child."

"Deep breath, *bébé*. Help is on the way."

I grabbed his hand and gulped in deep breaths as he did. "Don't leave me. You stay."

"I'm not going anywhere. Not ever."

When we got to the hospital, he stayed by my side.

"Too much stress and activity. You're not understanding restricted activity," Doctor Daigle scolded. "You need more rest." He put me on what he called complete bed rest. "That means you only get up to go to the bathroom. That's it for at least until your next ultrasound in two months." While I could sit in a chair part of the day, if my feet were elevated, mostly I stayed in bed.

I wanted the Littles to continue working on our homestead. To appease me, Armand hired his friend and retired Ranger, Oscar Lee, to help with the homestead and provide security when he wasn't there, as well as to be available for me when Armand was away on missions.

The Littles came over every Saturday. Over the next two months of strict bed rest, the Krewe and the Littles were able to mow the lawn with goats, although there was that small flower garden mishap that Bailey Marie was angry about. They even marked out the pond and rolled me out with a wheelchair to join them for a picnic there. After which, Armand hired a crew to install it and stock it with fish.

24

Securing the Homestead

Armand

Once the security system was up and running, it was time to run drills. Marc had also moved some pre-fab outdoor storage rooms onto our property.

When Renee saw the safe rooms, she frowned. "How much did all this cost?"

"I gave it to you at cost — wanted to see how the whole system fit together. You're a test site."

"And yet, not an answer to my question."

I wrapped my arm around her. "For you, nothing,"

Her back went ramrod straight. "That's not how a marriage works, Armand!"

"Okay, well ... I'm just going to go ... away." Marc escaped and headed off the others, so they stayed out of the line of fire.

Avoiding any sudden movements, I reasoned calmly. "Did you want safe rooms all around your property and a state-of-the-art security system?"

"No, I think it's too much."

"It's for my peace of mind, and you don't think it's necessary, so why would I force you to pay for it? Listen, Renny, bad people are targeting us. If Kayleigh is right and this is about Mr. Breaux's progeny, then you're carrying his first biological grandchildren. He's already made three attempts on the Littles', his children's lives. You think he will spare his grandchildren? You must be safe, Renny. I can't function if you're not safe."

Tears welled in her eyes, but she was smiling. "Aww, is that your way of saying you love me?"

"Show, don't tell. That's my motto." I grabbed her and kissed her.

"C'mon, that's gross. We deal with that enough at home." And Tanner had arrived.

I lifted my head. "Sorry, kid, you will understand when you get older."

Tanner left the room saying, "That's what everyone says, but it just seems gross to me."

Renee giggled, and I chuckled holding on to her.

Today the Littles were earning their greenhouse badge. Was this a real badge? Well, Ms. Ellie Mae would be sewing them, but I didn't know of any youth group that gave badges like Shell and Beau gave to the Littles.

They were creating a makeshift hoop greenhouse using PVC pipe, zip ties, brackets and bricks, and directions Beau found on YouTube. They had also collected egg cartons for the past few weeks. They were using soil dug out for other projects to fill them and then plant the herbs and vegetables for the potager garden that they were creating for Renee.

Marc put two fingers in his mouth and emitted a shrill whistled to get everyone's attention. "Before we begin, we need to run through safety drills." Then he had everyone running to safe rooms, turning on panic buttons and checking cameras to see if they saw any danger.

After what seemed to him to be endless safety drills, Tanner asked, "Do we get safety badges?"

"We could create one. I'm also working with the sheriff's office to offer self-defense classes. I could pilot that here."

Shell and Renee were whispering. "We want to take those classes."

"Can't while you have your buns in the oven. Don't want to hurt your babies ... or deliver them," Marc whispered under his breath.

"I heard that," Shell said. Her batlike hearing was legendary.

"—Alright, let's get a greenhouse built," I said, trying to distract everyone.

On the second Saturday in June, when Renee was cleared for light activity and I was back from my last mission, we all decided to have a homestead skills championship. The competitions included gathering eggs, building a bird or bat house, canning fruit, making pickles, and archery. Each child was paired with their *parrains* and both had to participate to win. While the ladies had lemonade and iced tea on the porch. It was relaxing and fun.

While we were competing, I opened a notification on my phone and saw that their perimeter had been breached. I pushed the panic button on my phone and called out to everyone.

"Perimeter breach!" I yelled. As Marc had trained us during our drills, the Littles and their parrains made it to the outdoor safe houses. I saw Kayleigh help Renee and Shell waddle to the safe room. They texted when they were safely inside.

> Renee: We're safe. Do you think they'll burn down Mawmaw's house? Like they did Gelly and Beau's camp?

> I don't know, but you should be safe even if they do. Room is fireproof and has separate ventilation.

> Renee, you have the video monitors. What do you see?

Renee: We're able to zoom in on the BGs.

> BGs?

Renee: Bad guys. We're calling them BG1 and BG2. Hold on, there's a button for me to send you the link. Did you get it?

> Got it.

Apparently, BG1 and BG2 were unaware of the cameras recording them. *Good help is hard to find.*

BG1 had his gun out. "I don't know where they went. They were all just here. It's those stupid chickens."

The guinea hens were creating a heck of a racket. Plan B indeed, Marc. I pushed the button to send the recorded feed to the Sheriff's office and to Marc's company.

"Let's just get this over with. Boss said to get the giant, Armand, the kids, and the pregnant woman and then make it look like a robbery. Priority on Armand, preggers, and the boy."

BG 2 said, "C'mon, let's check inside the house."

"You got the feed?" I asked Marc.

"Yes, and the ladies are all safely ensconced in the panic room. I'm sending the feed to my men and the Sheriff's office."

"What's going on?" Val asked, worried.

I patted her head. "Everyone's safe, Val. We just need to go and teach some *couillons* some manners."

"Beau, you got the kids?" I asked him as we made for the exit.

He nodded. "Yes, but teach them a lesson for me as well."

We left the children with Beau. Marc and I pulled our side arms followed the perps into *Mes Rêves*. It took a single bullet from each of us. While the perps had no qualms hurting women and children, they apparently 'did not sign up to be shot at.'

"You have to help us, man," the taller one said as he bled onto the floor.

"I'm sure help is on the way. They're glancing wounds. You'll be fine. In the interim, let's talk about who sent you."

"The boss doesn't like snitches," the short stocky one said as he tried to staunch the bleeding.

I walked over and put my boot over his wound. "You know what I don't like. I don't like little men who try to murder children and my pregnant wife."

They exchanged a look. "Who said anything about murder? We were just looking to rob the place."

"Uh, uh, uh!" Marc said. "Y'all better get your story straight." He played them the incriminating tape that revealed their target: Armand, Renee, and the Littles. It also exposed their plan to stage it as a robbery. "Attempted murder of a decorated Army Ranger, a pregnant woman, and children. You know where that will put you in the prison hierarchy? Right down at the bottom."

Armand sniggered. "What I think is funny is the loyalty you have to the 'boss' who didn't tell you that you were hired to murder an Army Ranger and his wife, as well as the adopted kids of a retired Marine. Did he let you know about that?"

"No, son of a bitch, said they would be easy pickin's," the taller one said.

"Did you owe him money, or was he just trying to get rid of you?" Marc asked him.

Sheriff Bradley Trahan drove up then as well as Marc's men and the EMTs.

Shaking his head, Bradley walked into the house. "I can't believe some *couillons* thought it would be a good idea to attack this compound. Do they know nothing?"

"We didn't know! Boss said it would just be an easy hit," short and stocky told them.

"Oops." I acci-purposely tripped and my boot landed on his wound. He screamed.

"My suggestion," Sheriff Bradley said, "is to cooperate." He tipped his hat as he followed the ambulance to the hospital to further interrogate his suspects.

The captured criminals sung like canaries. Apparently, their boss was a distant relative of the big boss. Bradley returned with a sketch of the underling boss. When Kayleigh saw the sketch that their artist had drawn, she froze.

"That's the *fils d'putain* my uncle wanted me to date. He's a bully and not the sharpest tool in the shed." She gingerly touched her cheek.

"Name, please?" Bradley asked.

"Stanley Breaux; he works at my uncle's casino. Not sure what he does, but based on his intellectual capacity, I would say bouncer."

Both Marc and Armand made a beeline for the door.

"Hold it, boys. Where do you think you're going?" Sheriff Bradley asked.

"To have a come to Jesus with old Stan," Armand said.

"Sheriff's business. You stay here and clean up. I'll let you know how it goes."

Twiddling my thumbs, waiting for word, was not in Roger's *Rules of Rangering*. I was pacing the house, climbing the stairs and checking every camera, like a caged lion.

Renee called from our room. "I can't sleep with you pacing about. Come to bed."

My pacing halted, and I peered through the door. "Your bed?"

She patted the bed next to her. "Yes, but just to hold me. I can't sleep."

I undressed as I made my way to the bed. "I can do that." Her baby bump was pretty evident, and I knew I was there for comfort, not loving. I rubbed her back and her feet. She drifted off, holding on to me.

In the morning, I brought her breakfast in bed. Well, what she could stomach for breakfast. Which is to say, hot mint tea and saltine crackers. That whiff of mint in the morning calmed her stomach and her nerves.

I hesitated, then plunged ahead. "It's time. Can we have the 'staying' talk?"

She sipped her tea, nibbled on a cracker, and nodded.

Sitting on the edge of the bed, I cleared my throat. "So, how have you enjoyed married life thus far?"

Wrapping both her hands around her mug of tea, she sipped. "It's okay. I don't miss going out. I do miss spending time with the girls. Although, I don't know if that's married life or pregnant life. I miss Choir Practice. I haven't done that in months."

"I can take care of that. Let's get you a girl's night out — or rather, a night in."

"Girl's Night? 'Night' sounds exhausting. With these two," she patted her belly. "I wake up late, nap twice a day and I'm in bed by five. It's like all I want to do is sleep and eat."

"What about an afternoon tea? With scones and cucumber sandwiches? It will be the middle of the day and we can plan it between your mid-morning nap and your afternoon nap."

"That sounds perfect. Wait, how does an Army Ranger know about high tea?"

"Actually, I learned from Marc. He has tea every Sunday afternoon with Sofia. He invited me a while back. It was a hoot. His mama, Ms. Sue, taught Sofia all about it."

"Yes, please!"

"And this can be all for you if you want. What do you say about including all the Littles so they can get a cooking badge? Then after they finish cooking the girls, and Tanner, if he wants, can join you for the first half hour. After that, it will be your own adults-only high tea."

She leaned back in bed. "I would say sign me up!"

The next morning, I contacted Marc's mama, Ms. Sue, and asked if she could teach everyone how to make scones, finger sandwiches, and what she called a proper cuppa. Being a worrier, I also sent Jeb and Kevin to our house as reinforcements for my friend Oscar, who was permanently guarding our *Mes Rêves* property. We never finished our 'staying' discussion.

25

Cajun Men Cook

Armand (again)

I met with the Krewe. I needed a reality check, and how! Etienne was finally back from D.C., so it was the entire Krewe, Beau, Marc, Etienne, and myself. We reunited at Beau's, just the Krewe, like old times. Shell and the Littles were with Renee at afternoon tea, being guarded by her brothers and Oscar. We fired up the grill and put foil around potatoes and cooked some John Daigre beans from the *Cajun Men Cook* cookbook.

Once we sat down to eat, the interrogation began, with Beau taking the lead. "How's my cousin?"

"Tired, grumpy, and pregnant," I said.

"And whose fault is that?" Beau tapped his foot.

"Ours, but I'm doing what I can. I try to do all the tasks that involve labor, but she gets even grumpier. Then she cries because she says I think she's an invalid and then she gets mad again when I try to comfort her because, as she tells me, 'She's not a weakling.' I swear, being pregnant is like being possessed by a demon. Someone is taking over her personality." I drug my fingers through my hair.

Armand glanced at the house. "Good thing Shell is gone because that would have warranted a flying shoe."

"Y'all, I don't know how to make it better. I'm doing all I can, but I'm pretty sure the second the twins are born, Renee, will be showing me the door." Closing my eyes, I squeezed the bridge of my nose.

The Krewe was silent, contemplating my dilemma, and eating our food.

Marc broke the silence first. "How are you wooing her?"

I frowned and finished chewing. "Excuse me?"

Marc took a sip of his beer and asked, "How are you courting her? Have you told her you want to stay?"

"I do her chores. I run her baths. I massage her feet and back. She even cuddles up to me in bed." I enumerated each task with a different finger.

Etienne snorted. "That sounds like sharing the burden. That's your job as the father of the twins. How are you courting Renee?"

"That's not courting?" I shoveled some beans in my mouth. I needed sustenance for this conversation.

Beau laughed, "Not even close."

"Well, it's not as if she wants to go out dancing. She's on restricted activity, for God's sake." Then they began launching questions at me.

"What's her favorite ice cream?" Marc asked.

"No idea."

"What kind of movies does she like?" Beau asked.

"The sappy Hallmark ones."

"And what is her favorite savory snack?" Etienne asked.

"Not sure ... *gratons* [cracklins/fried pork skin], I think."

"Well, there you go," Beau said, smiling and shoveling beans into his mouth.

I shook my head, "There, what goes?"

"Your date, *couillon*." Marc said. "Find out her favorite movie, bring her favorite ice cream and some *gratons*. Then you sit with her, eat with her, and watch the movie with her. It's not rocket science."

I shook my head. "Ugh, no. I don't wanna eat *gratons* or watch a sappy Hallmark movie."

Beau put his plate down. "Do you want a future with Renee?"

"Yeah."

Beau got up, straightening to his full height, and channeling pissed off Marine. "Yeah ... just yeah? You'd better be sure about this because if you woo her and make her fall for you —you'd best be in it for the long haul."

I stood up, giving as good as I got. "I know. Don't you think I know that, jarhead?"

Marc, the *brasseur de merde* [shit stirrer], Richard guffawed. "As much as I would love to eat pretend popcorn and watch you tear into each other, I think you're both on the same side — Renee's."

I sat back down. "Of course, I'm on her side, but I'm worried as well. This would be my first serious relationship. What if I screw up?"

Etienne joined in on the fun. "Oh, you'll screw up, no doubt."

"Well, I don't want my screw-ups to affect Renee. I care about her, and I want her to be happy."

Beau whacked me on the back in a 'somewhat' friendly manner. "Well, start from there. That's what the courting is for. To work out the kinks. If you aren't in it for the long haul, you can divorce her and just co-parent."

I nodded. "I hated that my father wasn't around when I was little. I mean, now that I know that Bill Breaux was the sperm donor, I one hundred percent agree with my mom. I was better off without him. Still, I promised myself growing up that if I ever had a kid, I would be there for him or her."

"Did you make any promises about the mother of your children?" Beau asked, his brows lowering.

"That I would never leave her and that I would always support her. I spent too many days watching out for myself while my mom worked three jobs to support us. I already told Renee; I would take care of her list of worries."

Beau snorted, "What is it with teachers and lists?"

"What's on the list?" Marc asked.

"A lot is about health. She couldn't afford the insurance when she had to go on leave without pay, so she was making do with general practitioners at express clinics." I pulled out her list that I kept. "I explained that I would always take care of housing and healthcare for her and that she could either stay home and focus on the twins or go back to work or both. I also promised to help with getting her body back in shape after, you know..."

"Let me see that list." Beau grabbed it out of my hand. "She's worried she won't survive the birth?"

"Something about the U.S. having the highest mother fatality rate of the western world. That one scares the crap out of me, but military health care has better numbers than the US at large. I actually looked it up. The US mother mortality rates are five times — 500% higher — than Europe, in general. In the military, they're only twice as likely to die. Still terrible, but unless I can get stationed in Europe in the next month, it's what we have to work with."

"No wonder she's so worried," Marc said.

"As a retired Marine, Shell used my healthcare for her pregnancies. One went smoothly and the second one seems on track." Beau's eyes scrolled down the page. "What about number nine?"

"What's number nine?" Marc grabbed the list from Beau and then whistled. He handed it to Etienne, who grinned and shook his head.

"Number nine is the sticky point. I'm pretty sure that happened when Renee fell asleep in my lap the first time we went out."

Etienne asked, "So, then, what's the problem?"

"I don't think that now is the time to tell her?"

Beau, ever his cousin's defender, asked, "Why the hell not?"

Etienne reached over and patted my shoulder. "You need to let her know."

Marc shook his head. "I disagree. You might scare her off. You don't need Renee running off pregnant, with a big target on her. Court her now and wait until after the babies to let her know. Beau, how long does it take for baby hormones to wear off?"

Beau chuckled. "I don't think they wear off; you just adapt to them."

"Great!" I said and rested my aching head against the chair's headrest.

"Improvise, adapt and overcome," Beau said. "If you were a Marine, you'd know that." I reached into the ice chest and threw some watery ice at him.

"Aw, see," Marc said, "They're starting to act alike, like an old married couple." I sent some ice in his direction as well.

26

Future Plans

Renee

Ms. Sue headed out with the female Littles; Tanner declined to join us for tea. Instead, to ensure his enjoyment and safety, Marc arranged a karate class taught by his men. Shell took that opportunity to ask Ms. Sue to teach the same lesson for Culture Fridays at her Académie Immersion School. She also asked if Marc and his men could take a Friday and teach self-defense to her students. Once she had them all on board, it was just us girls. Well, just us girls and the sentries outside, namely the ever-present Oscar, along with my brothers Jeb and Kevin. My other brother, Eric, followed Mrs. Sue and the girls.

We were served savory finger sandwiches, tender and buttery scones, and sipped fragrant tea, while we caught up on each other's lives. We each grabbed a seat on the porch and divided the food on the various side tables within easy reaching distance. Shell stacked a slew of quartered sandwiches on her plate that threatened to tip over. A giggle escaped from Kayleigh.

Shell stopped and glared at her. "What? These are tiny sandwiches and I'm eating for two, you know?" She then looked at my plate and guffawed. I had even more sandwiches and a variety of scones, with one of the scones stuffed in my mouth.

"Wha? M eashing for shree." I laughed through my scone.

Gelly, who was next to me on the porch swing, gave me a side hug. "That you are. Feed my little cousins, well, first cousins once removed."

Kayleigh sipped her tea and scanned me up and down. "How have you been feeling? Twins are not easy. We've had a few in my family. They take a lot of energy."

"*These* twins are in your family, Kayleigh," I reminded her.

Shell's eyebrow lifted. "Avoiding the question, Renee?"

At that, I rubbed the back of my neck and blew air through my lips. "Mostly Weltschmertz."

Gelly finished a sandwich and reached for another. I frowned at her skinny self. Oblivious to my envy, she asked, "Welts what?"

I leaned back in the swing and closed my eyes. "Basically, it's the depression you feel when your ideal world doesn't match your real one."

Kayleigh sipped her tea. "An ideal world sounds like a drag. It's too perfect. I'm more of a Stoic. It's not the world, it's how you see the world. Like Marcus Aurelius said, 'External things are not the problem. It's your assessment of them. Which you can erase right now.' My world is pretty dark now, but I choose to see it as a challenge rather than let it depress me."

Shell wiped her lips with a napkin. "Well, aren't you just a little ray of sunshine?"

Kayleigh shrugged. "Most days, I'm happy to just get by. I never have Weltschmertz because I don't want or expect an ideal version of the world. I wouldn't trust it if I had one." She picked up a sandwich and devoured it. Another overly skinny person who could eat anything. *She's your friend,* I reminded myself.

Then her words registered. Blinking, I asked, "Shouldn't you want to be happy?"

Kayleigh shook her head. "Wanting it and expecting it are two different things." She ate another sandwich.

"Well, I want it," I said, taking a bigger bite of my blueberry scone.

"I see ideals, like happiness, as goals, like what I'm working towards," Gelly said. "Etienne will be stationed somewhere. It won't be Meauxville, so I must make my dance school the best it can be and run it without being here. Is it ideal for the school, maybe not? Yet the challenge pushes me to think of solutions."

I paused, the scone halfway to my mouth. "Are you saying what's causing my Weltzschmertz could push me to creatively problem-solve?"

Gelly shrugged. "It's worth a shot. Now tell Tante Gelly your thwarted dreams, and I'll work my magic to fix them."

I shook my head. "Not so fast. I'm going to have to mull this over some. And on that note, I'm going to take my nap. Y'all can finish your tea. Gestating these two takes all my energy."

"I hear you, sister!" Shell gave me a high five as I rolled to the side and made my way off the porch swing.

"Good thing you have a big strong Ranger around to help with everything," Gelly teased, finishing up her scone.

"For now." I shrugged, making my way to the doorway.

"What do you mean 'for now'?" Gelly asked.

With a sigh, I turned to face her. "Like you said, he's a Ranger. At some point, he'll leave."

Kayleigh finished chewing her sandwich. "Not for good, just for work. I mean, you were planning to be a single mom — not like this threw a wrench into your plans."

"Yes, but now that I've seen how nice it is to have a partner, I don't want to give him up."

Kayleigh stood and hugged me. "Then don't. Keep him on. Frankly, it's probably more of a hassle to divorce him than to keep him around. You should keep him for the sheer ease of it."

I snorted a laugh.

"I agree," Armand said, firm and steady, from the porch steps.

I rolled my eyes and shook my head. "Going to bed. Y'all can try to plan my future while I'm gone, but chances are I won't be amenable to your plans."

Armand leaned down, his voice warm, and for my ears only. "I think you would be very amenable to my plans for you." Blushing crimson, I beat my retreat. Once I got to my bedroom-parlor, I tossed and turned, waiting for Armand to join me after our guests had left. For the past month, his presence brought me peace. As soon as he slid under the sheets, sitting next to me, I'd put my head on his shoulder. That would be all she wrote. As I slid into my dreams, I felt him leave the bed and my last thought was that I hoped he'd return soon.

27

Broken or Recovered

Armand

I scanned the faces of the ladies in the living room. Time for some small talk. "Did you ladies enjoy your tea?"

Shell ignored my efforts at small talk and pinned me with her teacher look. "Are you staying married to Renee?"

Looking each of them in the eyes, I was honest. "I will stay as long as she lets me. So far, that's until the babies arrive and then at least a year after. Once she gets a clean bill of health. I'm not sure of her plans."

Kayleigh leaned back on chair. "So, once she can take on all the tasks of being a mother by herself, you vamoose?"

My throat felt scratchy, and I cleared it. "If that's what Renee wants, yes."

Gelly tilted her head and stared me down. "And if that's not what she wants?"

With a shake of my head, I turned. "I'm still ... I'm still broken. She might be better off without me. I'll *always* support her and make sure she has whatever she needs. I'll do what's best for Renee, whether she appreciates it or not. Let me walk you ladies out."

I ushered them outside and as we waited on the porch, there was silent communication going on that I wasn't a party to. Relief washed over me once I saw the lights of Beau's new family SUV. His family was growing so quickly he only used Big Betsy, his old truck, as a farm truck now. Beau pulled into the drive, opened the side door and helped the ladies in. He took particular care with Shell and their soon to be fifth child. Gelly turned to me before she got in.

"I get it, Armand. I'm broken, too." I glanced at her scars. The ones she got helping to save Beau and Shell's oldest children from a fire. "Word of advice?" I nodded because I needed advice. "Just because you're broken doesn't mean you're unlovable. Don't make decisions that aren't yours to make."

It was a bit cryptic as advice, but I would think about it later. For now, I waved goodbye to the ladies and headed in. I had my medical and psychological eval tomorrow. That was another piece of the puzzle. I wasn't just broken; I also might still be a soldier. Army wives didn't have easy lives. Part of me really hoped I would pass. Part of me wondered if it would be better if they put me out to pasture. The Army was the only job I ever had, and I didn't know what else I could do. I had purpose in the Army, but if I continued being a soldier, would Renee still let me stay? These were all problems for another day. Right now, I just need Renee snuggled up next to me and to forget, for a moment, everything else.

I rushed to our bedroom, undressed, and pulled Renee into my arms. She faced away from me, her head on my shoulder and my body spooned around her. The thought of her letting me go squeezed my heart, but it wasn't my decision to make.

The next morning, I woke up, snuck out of bed, and looked down at Renee one more time before I headed out. She needed her sleep, but her adorable snores made me smile. All rumpled with flower-scented hair, I wanted to jump back in bed, but I had work to do. I headed to the kitchen and opened the side-door to Jeb. He was watching over the farm while I drove to Fort Johnson in Northern Louisiana for my evaluations.

I knew my shoulder was 100% or nearly. I'd been doing therapy on it for months. My only worry was the aphasia. Like the doctor had said, it seemed to have nearly completely gone away. Occasionally, I would have a repeated word, but it was rare. My physical was completed by a team of doctors. I for sure aced it. Dr. Hidalgo, my original speech therapist from Walter Reed, would be doing my psych/speech eval. I entered her office and sat opposite her.

"How are you doing, Armand?" she asked. *Excellent, an easy question first.*

"I'm feeling 100% I've been training, and I keep doing the singing training for the aphasia, but it's been a while since I had a noticeable speech incident."

"But you still have them?" She wrote a note down in her notepad.

Stay calm Armand. "I repeat sometimes, but it's rare, and it never frustrates me or interferes with the meaning of what I'm saying."

"You think you're ready for duty and that you can perform under extreme conditions?"

I considered a moment. My team depended on me, and I didn't want to put them in harm's way. I nodded. "Yes."

She scribbled in her notepad and then looked me straight in the eyes. "Scuttlebutt is that you got a civilian pregnant, that you're now staying with her at her grandmother's house."

This was an unexpected turn to my wellness evaluation. "You're amazingly well informed, yes."

Her eyebrow raised. What is it with women and eyebrows? "You ready to leave them behind?"

"I'm ready to do my duty and return to service."

She made some more scribbles. "Have you discussed that with your wife?"

"Uh ... Amazingly well-informed."

She nodded absently and continued writing. "I have access to all your paperwork. It's interesting that your wife didn't visit you when you were injured."

"She didn't know I was hurt."

Dr. Hidalgo glanced up at that. "She wasn't your contact person?"

Don't fidget, Armand. Stay calm. "She is now, but when I left on my last mission, I kept my mom as my contact. May I ask what this line of questioning has to do with me returning to active duty?"

She cocked her head to the side. "Just want to make sure that's what you're doing. We don't need soldiers who are using the Army to run away from their responsibilities."

I frowned at her. "I assure you. I'm not doing that."

Dr. Hidalgo nodded. "I withhold my judgement on that. For now, I'm signing off on your returning to active duty. Make sure you have your affairs in order for your new wife and child."

"Roger that." With a huge breath, I shook Dr. Hidalgo's hand and headed out the door. I had my job back. Now I just needed to speak with Renee and make sure this wouldn't destroy what we had built.

The moment I arrived home from the eval, I needed to pack for training. Renee met me at the door and gave me a big hug. "Well, how did it go?"

"I'm back on active duty."

She kissed my cheek. "That's what you've been working for. I'm so proud of you, Armand. What's next?"

I held her hand and walked her to our room. "I have two weeks of training at Fort Moore to meet my new team, then I'm taking all my leave time until you have the twins." He patted my stomach.

"And after that?"

I pulled out my duffle and began packing it. Not looking at her, I answered, "After that, it's up to you, Renee."

"I don't want to leave Meauxville."

I kept packing and just shook my head. "You don't need to leave Meauxville. I can come visit."

I could hear her pacing behind me as I pulled out everything that I needed. "That would be hard on you."

Turning, I grabbed her shoulders and pulled her in for a hug. "It's not a hardship to visit you and it won't be a hardship to visit the twins, and all my friends are here."

Into my shoulder she mumbled, "But us moving to Georgia would make your life easier."

I pulled back and scanned her. "I would love having you and the twins near me. I want to be a good father, Renny."

Her brow furrowed. "I have to think."

"Of course you do. You wouldn't be my smart little Valkyrie if you didn't battle with every idea that isn't your own. But listen, I'll be gone for two weeks. Your brothers will be taking turns watching over you. I don't want you anywhere by yourself. Oscar Lee will stay in the studio in the barn. He'll be here all the time. He can also escort you if you need to go anywhere. Consider him your bodyguard and personal driver."

The *tête dure* Babineaux came to the fore. "I can drive myself where I need to go."

"Yes, but the front seats are more dangerous. You'll notice that Shell and the Littles never sit in the front seat of their SUV. Can you at least promise me that you will let Oscar stay and that you'll let him drive you if you need to leave the property? Can you promise me that? For my peace of mind."

With a pout, she acquiesced. "Fine, I promise. Please note that I really don't like being treated like a child."

I zipped up my duffle. "Noted, but I'm not treating you like a child, just like someone precious. There is still someone out there with ill intent, and if we're correct, these babies might also be at risk. If Mr. Breaux finds out about me, then our children will also be on his hit list."

"I promised already, didn't I?" She was adorable when she grumbled.

"Yes, you did. Thank you. Why don't you have your friends over while I'm gone? What do you teachers call it?" Lifting my duffle, I headed to the kitchen. I had already laid out all the paperwork for her to sign.

Renee followed in my wake. "Choir practice. It's our Friday chill time, but really Kayleigh and Shell are planning my baby shower."

"That sounds like fun. Let me know how the baby shower goes." I handed her the papers. "Sign these," I said, then kissed the breath out of her.

After kissing me back, she pulled away. "No, you don't buddy. Fool me once, shame on you, fool me twice, shame on me. What are these papers?" Holding the papers up, she frowned at me.

I chuckled. "I'm not secretly marrying you again. They're just my legal paperwork, information about my will. You know, the usual."

Her brow wrinkled. "I thought you were just training."

"It's just normal paperwork. I promise. I must fill them out to restart active duty and for deployment." She skimmed the documents and then signed them all. I kissed her on top of her head and then went outside to stow my gear in the Challenger and greet Oscar. I was entrusting him with Renee's safety when I was gone, so I needed to make sure everything was ready.

I had to get to Fort Moore by tomorrow afternoon. Everything was in order. The systems were in place, but Renee was anxious. It would have been easier to leave right away and get to Fort Moore early. But Renee needed to be held and reassured. Instead, we spent the day together and I held her until she fell asleep. I left in the middle of the night. It would be a long eight-hour trip to Georgia.

28

Baby Shower Birth

Renee

After Armand departed, I was left to the tender ministrations of my overprotective brothers and the constant surveillance of Lieutenant Lee, aka Oscar. For the most part, it was uneventful — except for one Saturday when everyone but me rushed to the hospital to welcome Beau and Shell's fifth child, Ellie Denise Babineaux. I had to video chat with her from bed. Ellie D. was adorable and I couldn't wait to greet my own. One look at their squirmy little pink bundle of joy and my biological clock kicked into high gear.

Luckily, today was my baby shower. Shell, having recovered quickly, came over early and was writing numbers in a Sharpie on the bottom of rubber duckies as Oscar blew up the little baby pond for them in the parlor.

"What can I do to help?" I asked.

"Nothing, you're the guest of honor. Have a seat. Ms. Amelie!" she called to the kitchen.

My mama came out. "You ready for breakfast, baby?"

I was going to say, 'no', but then my stomach grumbled. Hungry twins. "What are you making?"

"Today we're eating all the interesting combinations I've seen you eat throughout gestation."

Oscar looked over from his task. "What exactly is on the menu today, Ms. Amelie?"

"For breakfast, pancakes with peanut butter, Zapp's Crawtator potato chips, and semi-sweet dark chocolate sauce. For snacks, we have vanilla ice cream with relish, grilled cheese sandwiches with pickles, Zapp's Voodoo chips, and ketchup. Finally for dinner, Pizza Village vegetarian pizza, to which we will add anchovies, pineapples, and capers."

"Yummy! Best menu ever!" I exclaimed, and I hugged my mom.

Oscar was on his phone, texting.

"Do you want some pancakes, Oscar?" Mama asked him.

Oscar shuddered. "Ah ... no thank you, ma'am. Kevin is bringing me food for the day."

"Suit yourself," I chimed and made my way to the kitchen. "You don't know what you're missing."

The baby shower was a blast. We would pull a ducky and whoever's number was on the bottom got a prize. We played the blind diaper game, which was harder because we were going with the reusable diapers. I opened all my gifts, and then we finished with the baby name game. Since Armand and I hadn't named the twins yet and we didn't even know their gender, we needed ideas. Each team had one minute to come up with ten boy names and girl names.

"Remember, we want traditional Louisiana French names. I'm not naming either of my kids Chester," I joked with them.

When they finished, Armand and I had a slew of names to choose from. For girls, my favorites were Amelie, which I'm pretty sure my mom put in the mix, and Aida for Mawmaw, which, if I had a girl, was a sure thing. For the boy names, my favorites were Beauregard. I've always loved my cousin's name, and it was a family name, as we both shared a great grandfather named Beauregard Babineaux. Then a bunch of saint names: Louis, Stephen, Vincent, Luc, and Jean, etc. I took a picture of all the names and texted them to Armand.

> If we have boys or at least one boy, I wouldn't mind naming him after one of the Krewe

> Armand: and for a girl?

> Aida for Mawmaw for sure.

> Armand: That's what I thought. Miss you!

> I miss you too.

I was smiling at my phone and the entire group said, "Aww...". I rolled my eyes and happily yawned.

My mama clapped her hands. "Well, that's our cue to head out. Our soon-to-be mama needs some shut eye. Thank you, everyone for coming. Kayleigh and Shell, why don't you carry those presents to the bedroom? I'm sure y'all have some catching up to do."

Kayleigh barely spoke as she carried my presents. She wouldn't make eye contact, and we had to twist her arm to even get her to show up. When she finally turned to us, we saw she had lost weight, and her makeup covered dark circles under her eyes.

"Nope. You're not going to do this. You're going to tell us what's wrong." Shell's fist went to her hips, a sure sign that Kayleigh could not get out of answering.

Kayleigh lifted a shoulder but kept her face averted. "I haven't been sleeping well."

I snorted. "You suck at lying. Tell the truth and shame the devil." I channeled Mawmaw, and Kayleigh smiled.

Kayleigh indicated my brother Kevin and Oscar, who were eating in the kitchen when we passed them with her eyes and switched to French. "*J'ai perdu mon apartement.*"

I saw Kevin start to text on his phone, and I didn't have the heart to let Kayleigh know that all my brothers were fluent in French. I tried to get her to stay the night. She could stay as long as she wanted, but she refused.

"I've got this handled. Don't worry about me. I'll figure it out." She gave me all the necessary reassuring platitudes, but they did not keep me from worrying.

Armand called the next Saturday. It had been pretty boring at the house alone, with just my guards for company. I looked forward to catching up, but he was all business. I was about to tell him about my worries for Kayleigh, but he stopped me.

"I have a mission, Renny."

Fear knotted in my gut. "Already? You were just going to train."

"That's how it works. Missions come up at any time. I just wanted to say, I care for you and when I'm back, we'll talk."

Keeping my breathing steady and my voice calm, I said, "I care for you as well. Be careful. No hospitals!"

He huffed out a laugh. "I'll do my best. Can you put Oscar on the line?"

I handed the phone to Oscar, who just kept saying, "No problem."

I cried myself to sleep every night for three weeks, worrying about Armand, wondering if I could deal with this full time. A month before my due date, I woke up achy. I looked down, saw blood, and screamed bloody murder.

Oscar came running up the steps. When he saw, he made a call, lifted me up and carried me to the SUV. He laid me down in the back and rushed me to the hospital. When I arrived, my obstetrician, Dr. Daigle, was there, and they rushed me to the back. All I remember was that they hooked up the monitor, and he said, "Two heartbeats." Then they put me under.

I woke up to pain and the smell of disinfectant and the sound of a heart-rate monitor. Armand was holding my hand and was asleep with his head next to me on the mattress.

29

Les noms [The Names]

Armand

My hands brushed a golden lock away from her face. She woke up and smiled. "You're back."

"I'm back." Then her mind cleared, and she stiffened. "The twins."

"Healthy and fine. It's you that did not have a good time of it."

"Where are they?"

"In NICU."

"You said they were healthy."

"They're healthy and scored a good strong eight on the APGAR, but they were tiny because they were a little early. They're nearly at the weight to allow us to leave with them. At least I can. You might be here a little longer."

"What happened?"

"You had significant blood loss and a reaction to the anesthesia."

"See, if we had been in France, they would have used a regional anesthesia rather than putting me under. Plus, they would have given me a mid-wife for before the birth and to take care of me when I get home. See, this is what I meant about the U.S. maternal death rate."

I dragged my hands through my hair. "Don't think those stats didn't torment me this past week."

"Wait! I've been out a week!" She tried to sit up but immediately regretted the abrupt motion.

"A week. You missed the fireworks for the fourth. I completed the mission three days ago. When I got back, I had a million messages and my CO got me on a plane back here. You scared me to death, Renny. Here, have some water." I held the cup and moved the straw to her lips.

She batted my hands away. "I'm ok now." She tried to take the cup, but it nearly fell out of her hands. Then she nodded that I could hold it while she sipped.

"No, I've been reading up. You're still in danger for another year. We're getting in a live-in mid-wife to help you with the babies and to monitor your health."

She shook her head. "I don't need that."

I set the cup down and folded my arms across my chest. I could be as *tête dure* as any Babineaux. "Well, I do."

She huffed and laid back in the bed. "I'm perfectly capable of taking care of myself. You'll be away a lot of time and not even living with us—" She motioned for the cup.

Softening my voice, I kissed her cheek as I handed her the cup. "—Your choice, Renny. If I had my druthers, I would always be available to take care of you."

"Oh, yay! I'm an obligation — my life's goal." She threw some wet ice at me, but missed, only underlining how poorly she felt. "Fine, as you're obliged to take care of me, you can stay, but I'll be downstairs, in Mawmaw's old room, and you can take your upstairs room back."

This was not the reunion I imagined. I shook my head. "Not gonna happen. If you don't want me in the room, I'll sleep outside the door on the floor."

"Look, let's not fight about this now. Just take me home, but first I want to see my babies."

I buzzed for the nurse. "Our babies, we have to name them."

Renee's eyes widened. "I didn't even ask. Boys or girls."

I rubbed my hands together. "You cooked one of each. The doctor won't release you until Friday at the earliest."

She shooed me out the door. "Then head to Beausoleil Books and get a children's name book. If we're going to argue, it might as well be productive."

I headed towards the door and stopped. "I'll be back. Any food requests?"

She grinned. "Raising Cane's half lemonade, half iced tea, please."

"Your wish, princess." I genuflected and headed out the door.

S he had been sleeping since I arrived. The nurse had brought in both twins and I had one in each arm as I quietly sang to them, kissing them throughout the song. I heard her stir, but I needed to finish my song.

She cleared her throat, but her voice came out scratchy. "I knew the singing helped with your aphasia, but I didn't know you had an amazing voice. That's one of the few French songs I know all the words to. *Arbre est dans ses feuilles*, right?" I handed her some ice water. Her eyes focused on me and then the twins. She cleared her throat again and grabbed the water.

On the night stand next to her bed, I had left the baby name book. Her eyes widened, and she reached for the book. Bad idea. She groaned in pain.

"Hold on. Let me get that for you." I laid our children in their beds and handed her the book.

She grinned and flipped through the pages. "You found a baby name book?"

"I found us a great baby name book." I held her cup with lemonade/tea in front of me. "Take a sip. You need hydration if we're going to break you out of this place."

She read the title. "*L'officiel des prénoms*. Aww, it's a French baby name book. I wish they had a book specific to Louisiana French, but this will do. I see you have some post-its in it already. What are the names you're thinking about?"

Sitting in the chair beside her bed, I got out my own lemonade and took a slug. "For our little girl, Aida, for Mawmaw Babineaux. Since she was so important to you, to us, really. Also, it's a family name on my mama's side, so it counts as a two-fer. Then I was thinking, Amelie, your mama's name."

She beamed. "That works."

"Plus," he continued. "Thing 1 was first born, and it was a girl so we could do our kids in alphabetic order. Both of those names start with an 'A'. Now for Thing 2."

She puckered her lips and laid back in her bed. "Okay, you can't call our kids Thing 1 and Thing 2."

"Why not? Those are great Dr. Suess names. Anyway, for Thing 2, the boy, I was thinking something like Beauregard. What about that? I wanted to name him after someone in the Krewe and since Beau gave me a chance and did not beat me to a pulp when he found out what we'd done, I think he has earned that honor."

"Someone not beating you up is no reason to name a child, but I do love Beau, and I've always loved his name. I love all those names." She lifted hesitantly to reach for her lemonade tea. I stopped her, set my drink down, and adjusted the hospital bed to the seated position. She patted my arm, reached for her drink and took a big gulp. "Umm... just lemonade. That's better. Let's switch." We switched drinks because what mama wants, mama gets. She continued, "For baby Beau's saint name, I was thinking Blaise. It starts with 'B' and he is a physician saint."

"Hah! I love it! High expectations. Are you up for holding them? They might be hungry. I could wait outside."

Her face was a sunshiny smile. "They didn't bottle feed them?"

I leaned forward and brushed a blond lock of her hair behind her ear. "That wasn't what you wanted. They have been feeding just not directly from the source, as it were."

"Give me Aida," I handed Aida over. She was so tiny, and she latched on immediately. Renee leaned down and sniffed her head. "Flowers and soap. Makes me want to cocoon her in my arms and protect her."

My mouth fell open, and I stuttered, "Do you need me to step outside?" She shook her head and gazed down at my little girl. "That's amazing. Wow, she was hungry." I picked up little Blaise and held him as she fed Aida. I gave a little sniff and the tension in my shoulders diminished. He did smell good, for now.

She caressed Aida's cheek with her finger. "Let's check to see if they like their names before we make them official." She leaned down and said, "Aida Amelie." Aida's free arm moved and Renee kissed her on the forehead.

"That one is official, then." I softly bounced Blaise in my arms. "So that makes you Blaise Beauregard." When I said that, Blaise whined about being hungry.

When Aida finished, we switched them out, and they soon fell asleep. Renee was looking exhausted. I settled both babies in their beds and rang for a nurse.

With her eyes closed, she said, "I'm going to rest my eyes for a few minutes. When do I get to go home?"

"Not today. You slept the day away and they want at least one more day of observation. Perhaps tomorrow, if the doctor allows it, but you will need help. I'll be around, but also our mothers have already each chosen a room in the house. They plan to be there for at least a month."

"That's nice." She yawned and then slept.

30

Morlocks

Armand (again)

> Journal Entry Week 1:
> Once I was able to bring Renee home with Aida and Blaise, the real work began. Week one was chaos but eased a bit by the mothers coming over and helping. Ms. Denise and my mom knew everything. I, on the other hand, was like a kitten underfoot. But not for long. Adapt and overcome, that's my motto. So, I will study each step of what *The Mothers* do and create my own systems. There will be some hiccups. Twins require constant adaptations. They work both independently and in synchronicity. I'm not saying they're my enemies, I'm just saying they're worthy adversaries.

"What are you writing?" Renee leaned over my shoulder and read. "You can't say our twins are worthy adversaries."

"I'm sorry, so when we were changing Aida, and Blaise began to regurgitate the milk we just gave him, how is that not an example of brilliant military strategy? I think you underestimate our children," I reasoned.

Renee guffawed. "And I think you overestimate their motivations. They're not out to get us."

"If you say so," I said, as Blaise's pee arched over the table and hit our fresh-out-of-the dryer clean diapers. At the same time, Aida threw her last clean *sucette* on the ground and started screaming bloody murder. "Well played, my children. Well played." I reached down for the *sucette*, wiped it on my shirt, and was about to give it back to Aida.

"What are you doing!" Renee said over Aida's caterwauling and as she reached to the bottom of the diaper stack for a clean diaper and quickly diapered Blaise.

I shrugged. "What? Five-second rule."

"No. That's not how it works. *Mythbusters* said the five-second rule only works when something dry touches another dry thing. The *sucette* was wet, you need to wash it."

I ran out of the room to wash the pacifier in the sink and ran back in. "Here you go, my little opera diva, a fresh clean *sucette*." I put it in Aida's mouth, and she spit it out immediately. It landed on the floor again. "It's not paranoia if they're really out to get you." I rushed back out to wash it, while Renee chuckled as she rocked Blaise.

When I came back in, Renee scrunched up her face. "You know this would be easier if we used disposable diapers."

I popped the *sucette* in Aida's mouth again and then walked over to hug Renee. "You wanted to homestead. Plus, those diapers just fill up our landfills. We just need to tweak the system a bit to make it easier. I've been taking notes when the 'Mothers' are here."

"The Mothers? Our mothers?" She tilted her head.

I shrugged. "You have to admit, when they're here, things run more smoothly."

"Are you saying I'm a bad mother?" Renee glared at me.

"What? God, no! I'm saying that we're learning how to do this and the best way to learn is for novices, that's us, to watch experts, that's them. Which is why, besides a journal of our progress in this mission, I also have started making lists of the systems that we need." Renee laughed as she rocked and fed Blaise. And it was the most transcendental moment I have ever had. *This is what I want!*

She looked up from Blaise. "Explain these systems."

Clearing my throat, I put up one finger. "Easy. The first is the feeding system."

Renee looked down at her breasts. "I feel like that one is self-explanatory."

"While you are the primary feeding system, you need rest. In addition, it's necessary to have a milk storage system and a backup in case the primary system fails."

She smiled and kissed Blaise's head. "Murphy's Law with me as the primary feeding system?"

"Exactly." I pulled out my notebook to show her my flow chart.

Renee snorted. "You made a flow chart?"

"I'm sorry, is this criticism from the woman who puts her books in how-I-want-to-read-them order?"

"Touché. Explain the system."

I pointed to the chart. "This is my first one, so expect some kinks and issues, and this is a first draft."

"Enough with the disclaimers. Get to it." Blaise released Renee's breast and burped.

I grinned, playfully cooing to Blaise, "No comments from the peanut gallery. OK, the system is simple. After you feed the Morlocks."

She peered up at me. "HG Well's Time Machine reference or X-Men?"

"I adore you. X-Men — because they often smell like a sewer."

"Lovely." Renee held her forehead and giggled as Blaise spit up all over her.

"After feeding, you can pump until you feel comfortable. The extra milk will be dated and stored in the silicon bags. One day in the fridge and up to two-weeks in the freezer. It will last longer but it not only degrades, it also will no longer be meeting their needs since your milk changes as they grow."

Renee's voice softened. "That's not a bad idea. Sometimes one of them is hungry, but the other is not, and I go around feeling uncomfortable to make sure they're fed."

"See, my system is foolproof."

She snorted. "What is your backup system if something happens that I'm either sick or can't produce milk? Plan C, if you will."

I put my finger over her lips. "First, hold your tongue. I need you healthy and happy or the Morlocks will surely take over."

"Will you stop calling them that?" Blaise tooted, to which Renee coughed and started blinking her eyes.

I moved to a safe distance. "Most apt nickname ever. Anyway, the backup plan, Plan C, if you win a billion dollars and want to go on a girl's trip to Aruba—"

"—Now you're talking."

"I searched for the best baby food powder. This organic one is the best. I have two canisters — lasts six months unopened. Once five months pass, I could donate it to the St. Francis shelter and buy another five-month supply, just in case."

"Hmm." Renee contemplated that silently for a moment. "Tell me about your other systems."

"Still working on them. For now, we need to set this one into play. You can tell me each week about how it's going and if the system needs overhaul or a little tweak." I picked up Aida, who had been squirming in her crib. "Now I'll trade you Boy Morlock for Girl Morlock."

Renee started laughing, but we made the switch.

31

Valkyrie Victory

Renee

After two months, I was starting to feel better. I could walk and stand straight. I still had occasional episodes of dizziness, so Armand had insisted I walk around with a cane when I was going for any distance. He called it a walking stick, but I knew what was what. Today, my plan was to walk the interior fence line around the farm, rest, and then harvest what I could. Of course, Cleoma always came with me. She had been very protective of me since we rescued her, or rather; she rescued us.

Halfway around the fence, the guinea hens started making a racket, and Cleoma started to growl. I got out my phone.

"You made me promise to let you know when the guineas were going crazy. I'm letting you know now. Also, Cleoma is growling like crazy." I told him, scanning my surroundings.

"Where are you?"

"At the fence line directly behind the house." As I spoke, I saw a man barreling towards me. "There's a man, Armand. He's coming this way quickly."

"I'm already on route. Keep your phone on. I'm recording the call."

Since I had gotten back, Armand had put my phone on a leash that hung around my neck. For once, I was grateful for his overprotective tendencies. I locked my screen and gripped my walking stick. The man was shorter than me and appeared to be coming from a fight. His clothes were torn, and he had nail scores across his face. I held up my walking stick, and he slowed his progress.

"You're taller than I was told," the stranger said.

"Told by whom?" I asked, following his moves.

"I need you to come with me." He reached his hand toward me.

Cleoma growled, and I stepped back. "Yeah, no. Not gonna happen."

"You will or if you're not careful, you will end up like that little bitch, Kayleigh." He swiped at the nail marks on his face. "Can you believe that bitch turned down my proposal?"

The thwarted suitor, that's who this was. "Since you attacked her, I think that was a wise decision."

"Her last decision." The stranger lunged at me.

I swiped my walking stick across his face. He feigned left and then moved right. When he moved in, I jabbed him with my fingers in his eyes as Cleoma bit his thigh.

"God damned dog!" As he turned to kick Cleoma, I smashed his nose with the flat of my palm. He went down, and I just started beating him with my walking stick as Cleoma went in for the kill. I kept beating him, worried about Kayleigh, mad at myself for not forcing her to stay with us. I took out all my aggression on this idiot until warm arms locked around me and Armand's scent calmed me. "Armand, he said he killed Kayleigh! He said she turned down his proposal, and it's the last decision she will ever make."

"Shh ... I'm on it, *chèrie*." Armand called the Sheriff to go check on Kayleigh and send someone to pick up the piece of *merde* that I just whooped.

"That's my Valkyrie. You'll raise our twins to be warriors."

I wasn't feeling that powerful at that moment. I was just exhausted and worried about my friend.

"Text everyone. He came to kidnap me. Something has escalated." I hugged Armand close. When I heard the piece of *merde* groan, I kicked him. You know, just to be sure.

Armand texted the Krewe about what happened. "Everyone is coming over."

Then I panicked. They'd tried distraction before, when they attacked Gelly. "Where are the twins?"

"Oscar has them in the panic room." He rubbed my back.

"You know, when you first proposed that panic room, I thought you were overreacting. Now, I'm happy it's there."

He smiled against my temple. "It was a good idea, and Marc gave me an excellent deal. Actually, he did all the labor install for free and gave it to me half price. He said it was a prototype and I'm 'testing' it for him. But I think he just wants to make sure we're safe."

"Text him a thank you and ask him to stay with Kayleigh. We can catch him up later. I don't want her alone and if she's hurt, I want her protected."

Armand texted Marc. Then he looked up to see Sheriff Bradley Trahan, Etienne's former boss, heading toward us.

"Again?" Bradley asked.

"Hey, we're not the cause of this chaos. We're the victims."

Bradley looked at the unconscious man on the ground and back at Armand. "It looks like you beat the crap out of your aggressor."

"Not me, I wasn't here. My Valkyrie did that." Armand grinned.

Bradley flipped out his notebook. "Okay, Renee, what's the story?"

"He trespassed and told me I had to go with him. When I refused, he said that if I didn't go, I would end up like Kayleigh.

She apparently refused his proposal of marriage. He said it was the last decision she would ever make, and he lunged towards me. After that, I don't remember much. I saw red and then Armand came to help."

"She didn't need any help, but I'll be more vigilant. I don't know how they got past our security system. Marc's checking on that as well." Armand hugged me tighter.

"Well, let me know. I will take this *vaurien* in and see if we can find out more." Bradley said, cuffing and guiding the perp to his car.

"I'm not worthless," the *vaurien* countered. "Do you know who I am?"

"No, did me trouncing you give you amnesia?" I asked, lifting my walking stick. Armand stilled my arm. "You're a coward who beats up women. Where were you taking me?"

"I don't know what you're talking about," the perp said.

Armand turned to Bradley. "Did we forget to mention we have an audio recording of him admitting to beating up Kayleigh? It also recorded him telling Renee she had better go with him or she would meet the same fate."

Bradley held up his finger and listened to his radio. Then he got a text and looked at that. He turned to glare at the perp. "I don't need your recording. Kayleigh woke up briefly in the ambulance and identified one Stan Breaux as the man who beat her up."

I sneered. "Breaux? Bro, did you want to marry your cousin? That's just wrong."

"Second cousins," he grumbled.

"Well, Mr. Breaux, you'll be going to prison for trespassing, assault, and attempted kidnapping, which is a federal offense."

Stan smirked. "I'll be doing no such thing. You get on the phone with Mr. Bill Breaux or you'll lose your job, Sheriff."

"I'm not afraid of losing my job, but Mr. Breaux only has one vote. There are a number of other constituents who would prefer I don't let a violent offender off."

"Did I mention we're still recording? That sounded like a threat to me. Also, it sounded like he was implicating Mr. Breaux. That enough for a search warrant?" Armand asked Bradley.

"I believe it is. Send me that recording." Bradley grabbed up Stan and headed towards his vehicle. "Kidnapping, you say. I might need to call the FBI. I happen to know one of their agents is in town."

I glanced up from my phone. "Oh sorry, I already texted Etienne. He's meeting you at the station."

"Renee, you have to make us at least feel like we're useful." He winked at me.

"C'mon Valkyrie. How does a warm bath, a cold beer, and a nice romance audiobook sound?"

"Like heaven." He held out his hand, and I grabbed on, like I was never letting go.

32

Aftercare

Armand

I left Renee soaking in a lavender and eucalyptus scented bubble bath and called Marc. He was at the hospital, checking up on Kayleigh. The deputies that arrived let him know that Kayleigh's injuries were extensive, but not life-threatening. However, the hospital was being difficult.

"Did the hospital call her parents?" I asked.

"Based on the bug that I put up at the front desk, the parents aren't answering. Hold on, let me listen. Oh, crap, her next of kin is her uncle William Breaux. They're getting his number."

I paced the kitchen. "I don't care if we have no concrete evidence of his guilt. You gotta stop this, Marc."

"I'm on it. I'll call you back once it's resolved."

I clicked off on my phone and then called Oscar in. He brought the twins in with him and we went over the footage and saw it, the weak area. Someone had cut the power to one of the Wi-Fi transmitters. The transmitters that were hidden and installed by Marc's company. I trusted Oscar with my life. He had saved it a few times, and I knew Renee didn't sabotage the security system. There was only one other option. I texted Marc.

> I think you have a mole

Marc: …

Then he stopped texting. While we waited, I went over the videos again. Whoever sabotaged the system knew not only the location of the router but also all the camera angles.

> A mole who knew how to cut off your security system and all the camera angles.

Marc: I'm on that too. Just got into Kayleigh's room. She put up quite a fight. She's a mess and gonna be in recovery for a while.

> How did you get into her room so quickly?

Marc: I pulled an Armand.

> What's an Armand? What did I do?

Marc: You can ask Kayleigh Richard when she wakes up.

> You're so dead. How did you get a marriage license so quickly?

Marc: Where there's a will…

> You mean where there's a ton of cash?

Marc: I'm a capitalist. You know that.

Renee called me from the bathroom.

Gotta go. Renee needs me. Do *not* leave Kayleigh unguarded and find that mole!

Marc: Not a chance and the mole is already found. Just devising the appropriate punishment.

Wait on that. We might be able to use him.

I clicked off my phone and ran to the bathroom. "Whatcha need, darlin'?"

Renee called through the door. "The twins okay?"

"Safe and sound and guarded by Oscar and Kevin. He was running errands for his law firm when the call came in." I tried the door handle; it wasn't locked. "What do you need?"

"Nothing. I just didn't want to be alone. Can you come and sit with me?"

I opened the door. She was such a beauty. Her legs were too long for the tub, for most things, really. Except me. Not going there. Renee needed pampering, not a randy husband-in-name-only. Pulling the stool from the stand-up shower, I sat at Renee's head and began massaging her shoulders. "Rough day?"

"Actually, I'm pretty psyched I got to kick Stan's *tchu*. Have you heard about Kayleigh? Is she okay?" She sighed when I hit a tense area and breathed through the pain as I dug in.

"She's recovering. Something was going on with her before this happened. I wish she had come to us." I said, massaging harder.

"Easy, I'm not the bad guy." Renee laughed. "I predict that it was her uncle's machinations. We can ask her when she feels better." Renee stiffened, then asked, "Someone is guarding her, right? I wouldn't put it past her uncle to tie up all the loose ends, if you know what I mean."

"Marc is with her."

"Oh, that will go over well."

"Trust me. He won't let anyone near her." I moved my hands under the water and started to massage her back. Renee moaned and then lowered her legs and scooted forward in the tub.

"Tell me that's an invitation." I whispered into her ear. She nodded. "I'm gonna need auditory confirmation."

She chuckled, "Auditory confirmation. You're a hoot. Armand, please join me in the tub."

It took me about five seconds to undress, and I nearly fell three times. Renee's husky chuckles were not helping. I plopped in behind her. My legs circled her, and she leaned back against my chest and sighed. I hugged her from behind and my gaze swept down her body. Her long, strong body. Her sutures were pink but healing, and I grazed my hands over them.

"They're ugly."

"They're beautiful. Warrior scars to keep our babies safe."

She squirmed against me. "You're a nut."

"I'm crazy for you." I could feel her eyes rolling. Time for a distraction. I moved my hands up her torso, cupping her breasts. She wiggled against me, causing discomfort. Exquisite discomfort. One hand stayed, tormenting her breast and pinching her nipple as the other moved down her body to her core. My fingers found her clit, and her legs opened, dropping to the sides of the tub.

She used her knees to leverage her body up. "More," was all she said.

More she would have. "Turn around, now," I commanded. Renee turned her head and raised her eyebrow, scowling at me.

Right. Valkyries don't take orders. "Turn around, please." Her scowl transformed in to a smirk and she turned, putting her knees down on either side of me. My mouth locked on to her breast as my fingers readied her core for me. "Let's get you nice and pliable, Valkyrie."

I entered her with one, and then two fingers, feeling her inner walls tremble. With my other hand, my fingers worked her clit, rubbing and pinching. She pitched forward against my chest, moaning with each movement of my hands. I leaned my head down. "Feeling relaxed?"

Her legs splashed in the water, and her nails scored my shoulders as she squirmed. "Not particularly."

Stilling my hands, I asked, "You want me to stop?"

Her nails dug in deeper. "Don't you dare."

I redoubled my effort, listening and feeling for a reaction as my fingers explored inside of her, and brought her closer to the edge. When I felt her inner walls trembled, I leaned down and caught her shout in my mouth. My tongue licked in. She tasted of bubblegum.

Then I surged up inside of her and felt the vestiges of aftershocks on my dick. I moved slowly, letting her enjoy the dreamy aftereffects, until I felt her walls start to tremble again. I kept my rhythm steady, holding back my own release. She was almost there; I could feel it. I leaned down and said, "You're mine. Tell me you're mine." She came then, and she moaned, "I'm yours." Damn straight, you are.

33

Bienvenue Back

Renee

Ever have those moments when everything changes, but you can't figure out why, and if it's even a good thing? Since what I thought of as the 'bathtub incident,' Armand had been different. He moved from the cot into my bed without a by your leave. Which was really nice in one sense, and a tad annoying in another. He put some more systems into place again without mentioning the changes to me until they were in place.

Okay, I'll admit his new diapering assembly line in the mudroom was inspired. Our house didn't smell and he and Oscar took care of all the yucky things. I just pulled off the diapers, used the paper towel for homemade baby wipes, and put on a new diaper. Also, he put a raised boardwalk through the garden when I mentioned I'd been scared to go out there since the snake incident. Did I mention the Rube Goldberg-like pulley system he and Oscar created so I didn't have to carry anything back from the garden? All this between four more missions.

He would be back soon. I had asked my mama and Tante Denise to help me clean the house and make him some banners.

"Let's make him your Mawmaw's blueberry and banana cream pie," my mama said. Sometimes little things like that made my heart contract, and I missed Mawmaw so much. I hoped she could see the twins. The ones that she read to every night when they were in my belly.

"Do you think she sees us, Mama?" I picked up Aida Amelie, her namesake, and gave her a kiss on her forehead.

"Of course she does, and you will teach your little ones about their grand-mawmaw and French."

"On it. I've already told Shell I'll teach her Pre-K if my own kids can enroll for free."

"Which means you need to improve your French, young lady." Tante Denise said.

"I do ok, but I've been forcing Armand to speak to me in French for at least half the time when we video chat. Also, I've been taking the twins with me to the Little Big Cup French table on Saturdays."

"I bet they're a hit."

"They will be speaking French in no time. Plus, I'm fluent in 'aren't they cute' and its myriad variations in French."

"I bet you are. Here, you're on crust duty. Mash up these graham crackers and melt the butter. I'll mix the cream cheese, sugar, and Cool Whip. Denise, you make the blueberry filling and cut the bananas."

"On it," we both said and got to work. While we worked, I turned on KRVS. The *Festivals acadiens et créoles* had started and all my favorite bands were playing. I started taping my feet to the "Bosco Stomp," one of my favorite traditional tunes. This rendition was by the Lost Bayou Ramblers.

"You goin' to the festival, *chèrie*?" my mama asked, while she spooned the creamy confection she made onto the crust I had made and topped with sliced bananas.

"No," I sighed. "I think it's too early to bring the twins into public. I'm a teacher and therefore a hypochondriac. Too many germies for my babies." I tapped my foot some more and executed a turn once I put the pie in the fridge to cool along with the blueberry filling. I picked up Blaise and started to sway with him. I was too much of a dancing klutz to risk dancing with him, but he seemed to enjoy the music and the swaying. Mama picked up Aida and Tante Denise started dancing by herself and turned up the music.

When Geno Delafose and the French Rocking Boogie started playing "La Valse de Grand Bois, "I closed my eyes and swayed with the waltz. Someone tapped me on the shoulder. I turned, and it was Armand. A face-splitting grin on his face, he grabbed up Blaise and gave him to Tante Denise. Then he gave me a courtly bow, silently asking for a dance. I nodded. He pulled me to the living room, and we danced to the next three songs. I only stepped on his foot a few times, and he felt wonderful in my arms.

Armand

I was tired and exhausted and just so damn happy to be home. That's what *Mes Rêves* was to me. It was home. I opened the door to Zydeco music blasting in the kitchen. Apparently, Renee hosted *Fais dodos* [house dances] while I was away on missions. I walked in to the most god-awful cute scene. Ms. Amelie danced with Aida giggling in her arms, Ms. Denise was cutting the rug all by herself, and *ma chèrie*, had Blaise in her arms and was swaying to the music.

I tapped her on the shoulder. "May I have this dance?" I asked. Ms. Denise swooped in and grabbed up Blaise while I took Renee in my arms. A calm and a heat settled over me as we began to sway.

After three songs, with very few missteps, I pulled her towards me and just hugged her.

"Welcome home," she said against my neck.

"I'm happy to be home." After a few moments of stillness, when I soaked up all that warmth, she smiled, grabbed my hand, and pulled me back into the kitchen.

Ms. Amelie and Ms. Denise both took turns hugging me and welcoming me back, but my eyes, like a magnet, kept getting drawn back to Renee.

Ms. Amelie must have noticed. "I tell you what. I think it's time for the twins to spend some quality time with Mawmaw and Pawpaw. Why don't I take the twins home for the night and y'all can have some adult time and then head to the festival tomorrow and dance to some live music? It's good for the soul."

Renee bit her lip. "I don't know."

Ms. Amelie upped the stakes. "Don't you trust me with my own grandchildren?" Renee's mama was diabolical. She knew which strings to pull. "And I'm sure Armand here would like some alone time with you."

Renee glanced up at me. I tried to look as pathetic as possible when our eyes met. The corner of her mouth crooked up, and I knew I had gotten my way. "I guess it will be okay, but I will need hourly updates."

Ms. Amelie negotiated. "I'll let you know when they go to sleep, when they wake up, and when they eat."

Renee hesitated and then nodded. "Fine! Armand, take the twins into the living room while we prepare for their first excursion, *sans maman*."

I held both twins on the couch, kissing them, and making funny faces while Ms. Amelie and Ms. Denise worked with Renee to pack up all the accoutrements, as Ms. Denise called them, needed for an overnight visit. They were packed up and out the door within fifteen minutes.

"Now you two make sure you have fun. Go to the festival, go out to dinner, just relax. Remember, Father LeBrun is doing French Mass at 8am on the *Ma Louisiane* stage. Y'all could do that."

"Thank you, Mama." Renee said, not agreeing to anything. When she shut the door, she turned and looked at me. "Hungry?"

"Starving," I said and in three steps, I had her in my arms. I kissed her deeply and until I had to come up for air.

When we lifted our heads for a breath, Renee said, "We need to talk."

Words to strike fear into any man. "Can we talk later?" I nibbled on her ear as enticement.

Her head dropped back, and she gave me access to her neck. "Yes," she said, and I smiled and picked her up, carrying her back to our bedroom.

I dropped her on the bed, and she giggled when she bounced. As I ripped at my clothes, she kneeled in front of me and unbuttoned one shirt button. She kissed my chest, leaving a warm wet spot on my undershirt. This continued all the way down my torso. Frozen, I waited to see what she would do next. Once unbuttoned, she flung my shirt in the corner and undid my trousers. She pulled them and my boxers down to mid-thigh, trapping me there.

She grinned up at me. "Now, don't move."

Parts of my body would not comply with that order. She gave a hoarse chuckle, grabbed tightly, and pumped. My head fell back on a groan. Then she licked, and I lost my mind. She worked me over, licking and sucking. She would bring me to the fierce edge and then pull back with a gentle puff of air.

"Dammit, Renee!" She grinned at that, nearly imperceptible, a Mona Lisa smile. Then she built my desire slowly ... a touch ... a pump ... a long-wet kiss until I couldn't hold back. Release roared through me. I fell on the bed beside her.

She licked her lips and straddled me. "*Bienvenue* back." My best homecoming ever.

34

Festivals acadiens et créoles

Renee (again)

We woke up early. We planned to get to the festival for French mass. Father Lebrun would be saying mass there at 8 am on the *Ma Louisiane* stage. Festivals started at 9:00. Armand had already brought me coffee in bed. I sipped it and tried to gather my thoughts. We needed to talk about our future. However, when I got to the kitchen, Armand was already plating our breakfast and talking about the festival. Yay festival!

"Fine, we can plan our day, but then we talk." We headed to Lafayette for the festival.

"As you wish," he said. I snorted because one, princess bride, and two, that wasn't a yes.

"*T'es canaille,*" I told him, because he was sneaky, but not in a bad way.

"Right back at you," he said as he drove to Lafayette.

After mass, we got ready to dance in front of the main stage. The first band was *Feufollet*. They played "Jolie Fille," and we both cracked up as we danced because in the song both the man and woman are calling each other *canaille*.

After their set, we walked towards the art festival and the second stage. On the way, we saw the entire Krewe. Shell and Beau were behind the main stage under a tent with Alex in a fenced in play area. Mr. Herman and Ms. Denise were on child corralling duty. I caught up with Shell, and then we moved on to the art exhibit. Gelly and Etienne were at the art show, negotiating with an artist for his painting of a dancing couple.

"Isn't it fabulous?" Gelly pulled me over and gave me a side hug. "I'm going to put it in my studio. Also, Mr. Jule is a LeBlanc and a distant relative of Shell. Isn't that right Mr. Jule?"

"Yes, but very distant."

"Still means you're family, and he will be in town visiting relatives for Christmas. So, he is going to bring some work and sell it at my Christmas recital. Isn't that fabulous?" Gelly was dancing to the music from the second stage as she talked. She was in her element.

"That's great! We're heading to the *Mon Heritage* stage," I said as Gelly started two stepping with me. She kissed me on the cheek and we moved on.

As we approached *Scène Mon Heritage*, Armand motioned with his chin. "Hey, that's Kevin and Jeb, right?"

They each were two-stepping with attractive females. "That's them alright. Eric must be on twin guard duty." We walked towards them just as the song came to an end. I hugged my brothers. They didn't introduce me to the ladies because it was Festival. They probably didn't even know who they were.

"It's been a while since I've seen you without a child somewhere on your person," Kevin teased.

Armand fake glared at Kevin. "Shh ... don't mention the ins-tway. It was hard enough getting her to leave them."

I shove Armand on his shoulder. "I understand pig Latin, you know. I know the twins are in good hands."

He rubbed his shoulder. "Oww! That's why you have been checking your phone every five minutes."

"Don't make me hurt you." I warned him, and he laughed and pulled me out to the dance area.

Cedric Watson came on stage playing "Le soleil est levé" with his accordion.

"I can two-step to this!" I told Armand and dragged him onto the field to dance. We two-stepped to the music. Armand only smiled when I stepped on his toes.

"Thanks for coming out with me, Renny." He leaned down then and kissed me, right there in front of everybody. It started as a slow burn and then turned into a conflagration. When we raised our heads, we stared into each other eyes. Then we noticed that the music had stopped.

"*Tout fini*?" The MC asked if we were done. I blushed and tucked my head into Armand's shoulder as he proceeded to take a bow to the applause.

"*T'es fou.*" I shoved him with my shoulder and made the crazy symbol.

We returned to my brothers, who were cracking up. I tried playing nonchalant, but my cursed light coloring made my blush apparent.

"I will throw something at you if you don't stop," I told them.

"We know, we know. Personally, I think we should have gotten some credit when you brought LU to the softball world series. In the early years, you practiced all your pitches on us." Jeb raised his hands in surrender. I tried not to laugh, but a snort escaped.

Kevin handed us each a beer. "A little early, but I think you've both earned it."

I hadn't had a drink since the night the twins were conceived at Shell and Beau's wedding, but it was hot already at 10:30 in the morning in mid-October. Hot started early and ended late in Louisiana. We stayed and listened to Jordan Thibodeaux's *Priere*. I put my head on Armand's shoulders as the song talked about living your culture or killing your culture. I turned to Armand.

"I think we should raise the twins to speak French."

"You want to speak all the time in French at home?"

"No, I want you to speak in French with them all the time. I'll join in when I can."

"I can do that, but when I'm away, who will speak French with them?"

"Your mama, my parents. Shell, Kayleigh, Gelly, your Krewe and, of course, their cousins all speak French."

Armand nodded. "Let's do that then."

It was nice making a decision together. Then I was distracted by the applause as Jordan and Cedric welcomed Cajun superstar Zachary Richard onto the stage.

"Since I did not prepare to play, I'll have to take requests from the audience," he told the crowd.

I immediately yelled, "'Lac Bijou,'" as it was my favorite song. My brothers, Armand, and then the people nearby also called out the song.

"'Lac Bijou,' it is." Zachary told us. Then Armand swept me out to the dance area as the waltz began. The song about the birds always finding each other at the lake, and then one day one of them is gone. It hit me harder than I thought I would. I stared at Armand. His presence that I had fought so hard to push away was now intrinsic to my very being. A tear slipped down my face. Luckily, no one noticed because it had begun to rain lightly. We kept dancing. We saw Rob Perillo's festival weather report that morning, and we had our shrimp boots on, or Delcambre Reeboks. By the time Zachary finished the song, only the die-hard dancers were left to dance in the mud.

Armand tilted his head and asked, "Wanna get outta the rain?"

"Not really." We were soaked through, so it wasn't like we would absorb more water. We walked around the park in the rain, watching people scurry to tents and to their cars. After a few minutes of walking hand-in-hand, the rain changed from what we call an *avalasse* to a sunshiny mist. We made our way to the food court, and got boiled shrimp, fried catfish with crawfish *étouffée* on top, and some bread pudding.

I smiled as Armand inhaled most of the food. "Happy to be home?" I asked.

"Always, but especially now." We ate and enjoyed our stillness in the frenzy of the festival. I only checked my phone two times. I was very proud of myself. When we finished our meal, Armand disposed of the paper plates and we started heading to the main stage again.

Halfway there, the heavens opened. This wasn't just rain, but a full-fledged thunderstorm. At the first crack of lightning, we ran to Armand's car. I jumped in once he opened my door, making sure that all wet portions of me were on either the seat protector or the floor mat. Neither of us were new to the *Festival Acadiens et Creoles* mud fest.

"Now that I have you as a captive audience," I said. "let's talk."

Armand pouted. "I had hoped to distract you."

"Don't *boudé*. You did distract me a couple of times."

"Three time's the charm." He leaned in to kiss me, but I put my palm on his chest.

"Talk first, smooch later."

"As long as smooching is on the agenda." He grinned.

"Armand, be serious. This is important."

"Okay, lemme have it."

"Well, if you will remember, you said that you wanted to stay on as my husband for a year after the twins were born. We're a quarter of the way through the year and I wanted to ask what your plans are."

I shook my head. "That's not at all what I said. I negotiated from getting the hell out of your life, which if you remember was your initial goal, to you allowing me to stay in your life for the birth of our children and then for an additional year. That was the minimum you would allow. If you want to revisit that Renny, I'm happy to renegotiate."

"My stomach fell. You want to leave earlier? I thought you said that it wasn't safe for me the first year."

"It isn't safe for you. The year after giving birth is the most dangerous time for a woman. I was actually negotiating for more time, not less."

"How much more? Like another year?"

"I was thinking more long-term."

I pursed my lips, hiding a grin. "Well, I'll have to consider. What terms are you offering specifically?"

He leaned across and kissed me hard. "How about a monogamous, passionate, partnership—"

"—Partnership, monogamous ... I'm not disagreeing with the concept, but the terms seem clinical?"

"What would you call it?"

"Love?"

Armand grinned hugely. "Love, passion, family, friendship. We can have it all, Renny!"

"I will always love you, Armand. I always have."

"As a friend?"

"At first, as a friend. Then, more than a friend. Now, much more than a friend. You're mine."

"And you're mine." He pulled me over the console and into his lap. Challengers were not made for people over six feet to make out, but somehow, we made it work. Until we heard knocking on the window.

"Oh! Shit!" I said, as I met the grinning eyes of a Louisiana University police officer.

"Aren't y'all too old for that?" he asked.

Armand sniggered and settled me back in my seat.

"Sorry officer, we were about to leave."

"Something was about to happen," the officer deadpanned.

I chuckled. "Leaving now," I told the officer.

"Ready to go home?" Armand asked.

"Let's go home." On the way, I texted my mama to see if she could keep the twins another night. She was happy to oblige.

35

Swing Hit. Swing Miss.

Armand

We waved to Oscar when we got to *Mes Rêves*. Luckily, he was far enough away that he did not see me drag Renee inside the house. I had enough sense of place to slam the door shut. I turned my Renny around and cupped the back of her head with both my hands and devoured her mouth. She pulled away for a breath and to drag me by the hand to the back bedroom. We stumbled to our room, throwing articles of clothing as we went. I tried to get us to the bed, but Renee was having none of it. She pulled me down onto the rug in front of the bed and locked her legs around me. Then she rolled me onto my back and sat above me with only her bra, a delicate and delightful scrap of blue lace, and her panties, plain blue cotton. Feminine and practical, just like my Renny.

"Let's get this off of you." I moved to rid her of her bra and she rolled her hips, grinding against me. I shut my eyes and moaned.

"I've got this!" She reached behind her, undid the bra hooks, and then removed it, dangling it to the side. My eyes were laser focused elsewhere. She had the prettiest handfuls of breasts. As she leaned down to kiss me, I filled my hands and squeezed lightly. She must have enjoyed it, because she groaned through the kiss. I licked into her mouth as she sucked on my tongue. She sucked in rhythm to the throbbing of her core on my dick.

"Too many clothes," one of us said, I wasn't sure who. Renee lifted her hips so I could pull off my briefs and then she shimmied out of her sensible panties and flung them to the side. Skin to skin, we laid together, absorbing each other's warmth. My arms encircled her. Then my Renny kissed me and began to rock against me, her wet core slicking my member. It must have been hitting her at the right place because she sped up and whimpered. I reached between us, to find her clit at each forward movement. I pinched at it. My Renny was laser-focused on finding her release. Slide, pinch, moan, again and again, until finally she tensed and stretched, and unfurled. She released and let loose and then dropped onto me spent.

I slid out from under her as she lay sleeping on the floor. Picking her up, I set her gently on the bed. Then I pulled out my basket of tricks that I had stashed under the bed. The good thing about old Cajun beds is that they have intricate metal headboards and footboards. I took out four silk scarves and proceeded to tie up my sleeping beauty. Then I poured some of the massage oil and rubbed it over her body. She moaned but did not wake. Not until I began to massage her feet. We had been at the festival all day dancing, so I knew they were sore. I tried not to be too put out that the moan she let out when I massaged her feet was more intense than any I had heretofore elicited from her. Then her eyelashes fluttered, and she lifted her head. Tugging on her arms.

I dug my fingers into her arch and asked, "You want out?" She rapidly shook her head and lifted her other foot towards me as far as it would go.

"Don't stop." I grinned at that and finished my foot massage. Knowing my germophobe elementary teacher, I washed my hands. I even sang the ABCs so she would know I washed them long enough. She was chuckling when I got back.

"Act three," I told her and began by massaging her calves, kissing as I went up. Whenever she would moan, I would spend more time exploring that location. As I moved up, I skipped the best parts. At that, my impatient Renny squirmed.

"Get to the good part," she ordered, lifting and arching towards me.

"I'm sorry. Who is tied up and who is currently in charge?" Her eyes flashed at the word 'currently,' and I imagined myself tied up with her on top of me. Later. Next time. Then I began to kiss and caress from her head down to her chest. When she started to pull at the scarves, I decided to oblige her. I kissed down, nipping each nipple and licking into her belly button, and then my mouth found her core. It only took a few licks and nips, and she went off again. This time, I pushed inside at the height of her climax. She was throbbing around me. Lightning passed through me then. I don't remember much but the feeling after that.

I awoke to her tipping me off her and squirming for a different reason. I released her and she high-tailed it to the bathroom. I'm an idiot. This was supposed to be about her and instead, with one move, I made it all about me. When she came out, I was about to apologize, but she had a grin on her face.

"My turn," she said. Relief rushed through me as she straddled me to tie my wrists.

I woke up, and my wrists were unbound, and Renee was snuggled up next to me. I carefully rolled out of bed. I went to the back porch to see if my elves had done their magic. The bistro table was covered with a table linen and electric candles were set on the table. I went to the garden to gather some flowers and berries for breakfast.

When Renee finally woke up, it was to the smell of my *pain perdu.* The good kind made from real French baguettes from Poupart's Boulangerie. I sprinkled on powdered sugar and fresh whipped cream and the berries I had gathered next to it. I glanced over and saw Renee leaned against the kitchen door frame just looking at me.

"What? Aren't you hungry?"

Her grin widened. "Starving."

With my chin, I motioned to the porch door. "Go sit, and I'll bring out the food. Coffee is in a carafe on the table."

Her smile, as she passed through the kitchen, sent warm tendrils through me. I moved outside with two servings artfully plated and found her stopped staring at the decorated table.

She turned when she heard the screen door. "And what is this?" she asked. I put the plates on the table, pulled out her chair, and kissed her cheek as she sat.

"This is me getting you in a good mood. Notice all the projectiles have been removed."

She laughed at that. "OK, hit me with it. What do you want?"

I sat across from her, my beautiful Renny, and said, "You, just you."

"What do you mean?"

From under my chair, I pulled out a velvet box. Inside was a sapphire ring that matched my Valkyrie's eyes. "I want you forever, in my life. I want the good times, the bad. I want you gently and I want you tied up. I want you all the time in my life."

She leaned forward, her elbow on the table and her chin in her hand. "I'm gonna need a little more, Armand."

I shook my head. "You never make it easy."

She took a sip of her coffee. "If you wanted it easy, you would not be asking what I think you're asking, but you're missing some words. Three, to be exact."

"Always pushing, you *tête dure* Babineaux."

"Pushing for improvement. Now start over from the top." She made a circular motion with her other hand.

"I don't remember the words exactly."

She leaned back in her chair and crossed her arms. "Start over."

I grinned. "Renee, you impossible, hardheaded woman. I love you and want to spend my life getting pushed and prodded and dodging projectiles. Will you marry me?"

"Yes, and that was very well done." She held her hand up, and I put the ring on it. Then she cut and put the first piece of French toast in her mouth.

"And...?" I prodded.

She stopped chewing. "And what?"

"And you love me."

"Of course I love you, or I wouldn't have agreed to marry you."

"We're already married."

"Yes, but this time you have my consent and that makes all the difference." She continued to eat, and I smiled.

"That it does."

By mid-morning Renee had taken pictures of her ring and let everyone know we were getting married, 'for real' as she called it. My mom, Ms. Amelie and Ms. Denise came over with already elaborated plans. They must have been in the works for some time. They wasted no time, and the wedding was planned for the weekend before Thanksgiving.

Renee beamed. "This is our happily ever after." At least that's what we thought. I had proposed for real and we were planning our wedding. The most drama we had to deal with was a quick mission that I had to do and telling our parents about our plans. Then less than a week after the proposal, after a night of welcome back sexy time, disaster struck. Caught in a nightmare and thrashing about, I didn't think I was fully awake when Renee nudged me to stop moving. In my dream, it was an assault, and I shoved her away and off the bed. She wasn't hurt, Thank God.

At that instant, I broke free of the nightmare. "Oh, my God, Renny, are you okay?"

She got up gingerly. "I'm fine. Note to self: don't wake you during a nightmare."

I checked her over to make sure she wasn't hurt. Guilt strangled me and was no doubt etched on my face. Grabbing up the pillow, I went to the couch. The next night, I had another nightmare. I awoke to Renee watching me from a safe distance, not knowing what to do but wanting to, needing to help. With the thrashing, I landed on the floor. Renee approached to help, but I shook her off and jumped back. *I was unsafe.* Without a word, I went outside, spoke to Oscar, and five minutes later, he was knocking on the door.

"I'm here to make sure you're okay. Armand sent me."

Renee questioned him. "He moved to the barn?"

Oscar nodded, and she let him in.

Exhausted, I went to bed. I would have to deal with this tomorrow. In the distance, I heard Aida cry. *You know something's wrong, Aida, my darlin'.*

When I woke up the next morning, I made an appointment to see a shrink. With a text, I let Oscar know I would be back later that afternoon and that his job was to protect my family at all costs — even if that was from me.

36

Bourré

Armand (again)

Something was up. I felt it the moment Marc called to invite me to the Bourré game. First, Etienne was there, and he was supposed to be finishing up some more training in DC. Second, it was only us, since Beau and Etienne married all of our Bourré games had included at least one woman. Something was definitely up, and this felt less like a game and more like an intervention. When I arrived and Marc gave me a selection of Swamp Pops rather than LA31 beers, I was sure it was an intervention.

"What's up? And what's with the coke?" I asked, raising up my Satsuma Fizz with a questioning look.

"Have a seat," Marc said and shuffled the deck. He dealt us each five cards and turned over his last card. "Diamonds are trump. Who needs to change cards?"

I had a great hand. Ace and king of diamonds, ace of hearts, and two more smaller diamonds. What's that old saying about you can be either lucky in cards or love? As luck would have it, Marc led with a king of hearts, which I smacked with my ace and won the trick. "Again, I ask," as I slapped down my nine of diamonds. "What is going on?"

They threw out all their high trump cards, the queen, the jack, the ten. Beau won the trick with his queen. He threw out an ace of clubs. "We just wanted to see how you were doing, you know, with the wedding planning."

"*Ça c'est de la merde,*" I told them.

"*Merde* is a bad word," Sophia said from the doorway.

"It is honey. What can we say instead?" Marc grinned and asked her.

"*Ca ca* in French and in English," she said.

"*C'est du caca,*" I told my Krewe, who chuckled.

Marc walked over, picked her up, and kissed her cheek. "Why aren't you in bed, sweetheart?"

She hugged Marc back. "I wanted to say goodnight to the Krewe, and Ms. Kayleigh said she wants me to fetch her a Sarsaparilla Root Beer. You took all the Swamp Pops from the fridge."

"Okay, darlin', but then it's to bed with you."

"*Oui, Papa!*" She made the rounds, giving us each a hug goodnight, dug in the cooler for an ice-cold a Sarsaparilla Root Beer, palming a Praline Cream Soda for herself, and then scurried out of the game room.

Etienne nodded, impressed with Sofia. "Smooth snaffle. I nearly missed the second coke that she palmed."

Beau focused instead on what Sof had said. He raised his eyebrow. "Kayleigh is still living here?"

"I couldn't drop her off at her apartment. Ahh ... it wasn't an option. Besides, she needed care, and it's safer here than ... where she was living. She's been through enough."

"Didn't she recover weeks ago?" Etienne asked.

"She's safe and comfortable. Let it go."

"I will if you will." I took a gulp of my Satsuma Fizz. It's sweet tang, soothed my nervous throat.

Beau shook his head. "Not gonna happen until you explain why you're living in the barn instead of with your lovely fiancée, my cousin, and your two adorable children."

I explained about the night terrors and about nearly hurting Renee. "I can't hurt her. Ever."

"Of course not. You're a protector," Etienne said. "Actually, you really are more like an Architect."

We all groaned. Pop psychology, yay! I did not need that at this point. "What I mean is you need to protect and you need strategies and systems."

"I do like me a good system." I told them, "But my VA shrink only offered drugs. I can't be hopped up at all times around my family."

"Call this number." Marc handed me a card.

"Who is it?"

"A psychiatrist that specializes in PTSD and a particular therapy that's especially effective. It's called Eye Movement Desensitization Reprocessing. *Grosso Modo*, you watch some lights, especially in your peripheral vision, and you talk about what brought you to this point. Kayleigh hasn't had a nightmare in weeks since she started. I'm telling you, it's very effective."

"I can try it, but in the interim. I need to stay away from my family. They need to be safe." Then I set my ace and king down and won the pot.

Renee suspected nothing. I came back from the Bourré game in good spirits, helped get the twins ready for bed, then sat on the front porch with her. She drank wine, and I drank water. That should have tipped her off. We were both calm and relaxed, talking about our day. I showed her all the coins I won at the game and promised to bring her along next time. This was what I envisioned for our life. With her head against my shoulder, I enjoyed the calm and the lightening bugs. Renee's sigh of contentment transformed into a yawn. It had been a long day.

She kissed my cheek. "I guess we should head to bed."

I nodded, got up, and followed her to our room. When we got to our bedroom door, I kissed her goodnight. Like really kissed her. And then I pulled out all my duffle bag and started putting all of my things in it. It took a moment for her to register what was happening.

"What the frick, Armand?" She followed me to the door. On the way picked up one of Mawmaw's tchotchkes, one of the few her brothers did not take. She beaned me in the back with it.

"Ouch, dammit, Renee." I rubbed my back.

"What? I aimed for your torso. I know you're having head issues. What's happening here?"

"I'm sleeping in the barn." I turned and opened the door.

"I know that, but why are you packing up all of your things?" Her question ended in a strangled sob.

Closing my eyes, I inhaled, put down my duffle and turned. "Because keeping you safe might mean I have to stay further away from you and for longer time periods. I don't want to pose a threat to you or my children."

Sad did not sit well on my Valkyrie; it morphed into fury. "You aren't a threat to me, but I might be to you if you pack up and leave."

"Renny."

"Don't you dare call me Renny during a fight!" She scanned the foyer for projectiles.

"Are we fighting?"

"If you plan to walk out that door with all your things, then, yes, we're fighting." She picked up a vase from the entry table and dumped the flowers I had gotten her on the floor.

"My job is to keep you safe. End of story. Don't throw Mawmaw's favorite vase."

She narrowed her eyes at me. "My job is to love you in sickness and health. End of story."

I dragged my hands over my face. "I could have hurt you—"

"—You didn't."

"But I could have, and that's unacceptable." I picked my duffle back up.

"I could have hurt you when I launched that ceramic shepherdess at you. But I didn't, because I made sure I wouldn't."

"I can't control my nightmares —"

"—Yet. You can't control them, yet. But there are plenty of strategies we can use to help you."

"That's great, but in the interim, I'll be in the barn and Oscar is moving temporarily into the guest room to make sure you stay safe." Opening the screen door, I headed out.

"Don't walk out the door. If you do —"

Stopping, I closed my eyes, but kept my back to her. "—Don't, Renny, don't say anything you might regret. Let's just give it some time. A month—"

"—We're supposed to get married before that."

"Two weeks." I negotiated.

"One day."

"One week."

She stomped onto the porch. "Fine, get out, but don't expect any perks while you set up your household out there at the barn. I finally let you in my life and you back out. That's not okay, Armand."

"I know. I just need some time, Renny. I love you." I hitched my duffle on my back and made my way to the barn.

Renee's eyes followed me. Before I closed the barn door, I heard her say, "I love you, too, *couillon.*"

Miserable, irate, annoyed, these were all words that reflected my mood. I had started seeing that shrink that Marc suggested. Since it was time sensitive, she had me going every other day. It had only been a few days, but I already saw a change in the nightmares. I had more control, but it still wasn't safe for Renee. Renee also set up a 'visitation schedule' to let me know how things would be if I decided to make this separation permanent.

I visited the twins every day on the porch only. The house was off limits. Renee was there overseeing my visits, but she gave me the silent treatment. Wedding plans were halted, while I 'decided what I wanted.' In addition, the number of pinecones that hit me as I walked outside could not have been coincidental. The pine trees were not out to get me, but someone was venting her spleen. Did I mention the calls from well-meaning parents?

First, there was my mom. She called just as I was cleaning out the stalls and taking care of the horses. Since my hands were full, I had her on speakerphone. Her voice reverberated around the barn when she yelled, "What the hell are you doing, Armand?"

I kept shoveling as I answered, "Mom, this really isn't your business."

"I'm sorry, my grandchildren are going to be on a visitation schedule with my dumbass son, and you tell me it's none of my business?"

I shoveled faster. "We're working it out."

"Really? Work faster. From what I can see and have heard, you aren't even speaking. How can you work it out, Armand, if you aren't even speaking?!"

"I will work it out." The force of my last shovelful tipped over the wheelbarrow. I needed to start again.

"You better!"

No sooner had I placated my mother, when Renee's mama called.

"Good morning, Ms. Amelie."

"Is it? Because my baby girl is having to raise those babies by herself and is crying herself to sleep every night."

"I'm trying to protect her."

"Looks more to me and to Mr. Travis that you're shirking your responsibilities."

"She's being *tête dure* and won't let me help more."

"I'm sorry, have you never met a Babineaux?" Even in my frustration, my lip crooked up at that comment. I tried to respond, but she talked right over me. "That's not the issue. The issue is you can't work out a problem if you're separate."

"Look, we have to work this out on our own."

"Well, work it out quickly."

"I will, I promise."

"I'm not cancelling this wedding."

"Yes, ma'am."

"You love my baby, right?"

"I do very much."

"Then stop being a *couillon* and work this out."

"Yes, ma'am."

As I hung up with Ms. Amelie, a pinecone hit me in the chest. I turned to the house, and Renee was knitting in a rocking chair.

"Can we talk?"

"Are you coming back to live with your family?"

"You gave me a week."

"So, take your week and then we'll talk."

The next morning, everyone I knew was at *Mes Rêves*, but only my Krewe acknowledged me and they wouldn't speak to me. They just tipped their chins to say hello and went in the house. Then the construction crew arrived.

37

Fixer Upper Heart

Renee

The next morning, I opened the door to the construction crew as well as our friends and family. The Krewe was also helping, but I'd sworn them to secrecy. They were allowed to go and talk to Armand, but I forbade them from ruining my surprise. I watched them nod to him as they came through the gate, but other than that, they avoided him.

"Good morning." I waved to Armand, who was standing outside the barn watching the comings and goings of everyone. He waved back, then pressed his fist to his lips.

My mama and Ms. Rose pulled up with Kayleigh and Mr. Travis. My mama jumped out. "Let's get this show on the road."

I ran in and packed up the twins for them to watch. As they loaded them into the car, Armand gave a head signal to Oscar and he prepared to trail them. No wonder he was so stressed. He always worried about protecting everyone. I waved and headed back into the house.

We started the morning in the living room with coffee and planning. I doled out everyone's task.

"Shell and Beau are on greenery duty. Head to *Fleur,* the nursery outside of town. I'm think that we will need some lavender and rosemary for calming smells and some ivy to keep the air clean. Plus, tall plants are supposed to promote peace and a positive outlook. Perhaps get a tall Ficus." I handed them my credit card.

Shell rolled her eyes. "We will make a bagel run as well. Aurelie at Soleil Café is cooking up some fresh bagels and croissants in case we get hungry."

Great, I tried handing her my card again. They both just stared at me. Finally, I gave up and just hugged them. "Thank you."

"No, thank you. Now, we have our task. Gotta go, cuz," Beau said, as they headed out.

"Tante Denise and Nonc Herman. Y'all are on declutter duty. While this is for the entire house, please focus first on exit paths from any point of egress. That's the clutter that's the hardest for anyone with PTSD."

"We are on it, *chérie*. This is a good thing you're doing here," Tante Denise said. Nonc Herman just hugged me and it always felt so much like daddy because they didn't just look the same, they smelled the same as well.

I put Armand's Krewe on paint duty. Mawmaw's bright walls would be replaced with a calming palette of white and pastel blue with pops of pastel green to bring joy. Even the wood was lightened because brown, according to the studies Kayleigh sent me, sparked feelings of sadness and disgust. Once everyone else had their tasks, I spoke to the construction crew about fixing the big problem. It would require more and better doors and windows and actual construction in the house. It was a big job and I don't know how Marc was able to get me this crew so quickly and have them work all day, but he did it.

Everyone worked from early morning until late evening. Around seven, Armand knocked on the door.

"You can't come in right now." I told him.

"I ... I just wanted to make sure that you had eaten, and that you were drinking enough water. You've been working all day." He handed me a Pochés seafood plate lunch and turned on the porch radio, my favorite swamp pop song, Zachary Richard's version of "Un autre soir ennuyant." My empty evenings also made me want to cry.

"Thank you, I did forget to eat. This is too much for me. Come join me."

He stepped towards the door, but I veered toward the rocking chairs on the porch. I placed the container on the side table between the chairs and handed him the fork.

"You don't need a fork?"

"I'm starting with the fried shrimp and catfish. I'll use it later." I dug into the meal. I hadn't eaten but half a bagel that day.

"So, whatcha building?"

"Nice try. How've you been sleeping? How is your therapy going?"

"Sleep has been better and that treatment is helpful. I haven't had a nightmare in two nights. So, that's good."

"Excellent. So, you'll need to keep doing that therapy. Even once you feel better, you need to continue. Especially as you're not changing jobs and more events could trigger episodes."

"You want me to quit?"

"No, I want you to be healthy and happy. I know that this job feeds your need to protect. I just want to make sure as you are protecting everyone else that someone is looking out for you."

"And that someone is you?"

"I could be. I'll let you know when you can come over for breakfast tomorrow. The work is done and you can have a look at what we did."

After all the workers left, the Krewe went over to Armand. They each gave him a hug and told him to not be such a *couillon* and they left. I didn't sleep that night. I spent it straightening and organizing for the big reveal tomorrow.

38

The Big Reveal

Armand

The next morning Renee sent over a formal written invitation via Oscar.

"Next thing you know, she'll be dressing me in livery. I'm not a footman, you know." He handed me the envelope and turned to leave. "You have to go. She went to a heap of trouble for you."

I grabbed up the envelope and put it on my kitchenette counter. "I'm going. If anything, the curiosity alone will force me to go. I'm just need to finish my coffee, so I'll be on my toes. You never know when I'll step wrong and Renee will launch a projectile at me."

Oscar laughed as he walked away. "She does keep you in line."

I drank my coffee and opened the envelope.

> *Dear Armand,*
>
> *I know you think you need to be separate from us to protect us. But who's protecting you? I am that's who. In sickness and health, 'til death do us part. You are hereby invited to join me for breakfast this morning at nine. Bring your appetite and an opened mind.*
>
> *Your love,*
> *Renny*

I looked at my phone. It was 8:30 am. She'd put in the effort. I could match that effort as well. At 9 am sharp, I knocked on her … our door. I was wearing my best western wear: ironed jeans, western snap shirt, elaborate boots and wildflowers that I had gathered in the field. Renee opened the door wearing jeans, a tank, and one of my old button-down shirts. She was so bright and lovely.

Her eyes scanned me up and down. She grinned. "I'm pleased you made an effort. You're looking good."

"You, as well. What's this about Renee? And what was going on yesterday?"

"I think I have a solution." Renee took me by the hand and guided me into the house.

I braced for impact, but it never came. "It's different, right?"

My head swiveled back and forth. "It's different. What's different? I mean, besides the paint color."

"I'll tell you, but first you have to come and see my big surprise." She pulled me into our bedroom. It looked a little smaller, but pretty much the same except for the paint and a new door. "Go ahead, open it." She nodded to the door and was bouncing on her toes.

I turned the knob and pulled the door. Inside was pure peace. "How? Why?"

"Kayleigh sent me some research and told me what was helping her. The chair becomes a bed, if you feel the need. If you've had a rough day, and you think it might bleed into the night. The plants' smell should calm you, and they clean the air. The colors here and throughout the house were chosen to give you peace and a positive outlook. We also put in this sliding glass door so that you have egress but also more natural light. That again is supposed to help."

I reached for her, but she moved away.

"You don't have to worry. You can keep me safe and," she gestured to the house, "I will keep you safe and calm."

"It won't bother you not sleeping with me?"

"Oh, I'll be sleeping with you. We can sleep together for sexy-time, or any time. I want you by my side, but if you need space, if you think it might be a bad night, or if you wake to a nightmare, then you simply move to your room. It will be like we're to the manner born. This is the mistress bedroom, and that one is the master."

"You added a room for me?" I stared through the doorway.

"I did." She put her hand on my shoulder. "I want you back. Come back home, Armand."

Turning, I smiled, hugged her, and then lifted her as I turned in circles. When I set her down, she framed my face with her hands, and her lips fluttered against mine.

"So, you'll come back?"

"I'm already home."

$$39$$

I Do

Renee

S ince we were already legally already married, we just wanted a small ceremony for our friends, family, and community. My mama was not of the same opinion and what Mama wants; Mama gets. The plan had enlarged. I'd gone to Tante Em's store and picked out a lovely sundress. However, today I was back because the sundress had been downgraded to the rehearsal dress, and Mama's only daughter would not be depriving her of helping her pick out a wedding dress.

"How about this one?" My mama held out a Cinderella ball gown. My eyes pleaded with Tante Em and Ms. Rose.

"Denise, that's too much. Search for more modern clean lines," Tante Em told her sister. I mouthed 'thank you,' and she nodded.

In the end, I ended up with an A-line, floor-length chiffon with a gold corset on top. I figured since he called me his Valkyrie, I should look the part. I even had *Bijou* Jewelry create some arm cuffs and hair combs for me.

"You're going to knock him out," Ms. Rose told me. "He used to have a poster on his wall of a superhero that looks exactly like you. I will make sure to take a picture the moment he sees you."

"That's my goal. I want his jaw to hit the floor."

Ms. Rose said, "Thank you for inviting me. I never had a daughter. Just Armand, and he pretty much raised himself."

"Well, I'm your daughter now." I gave Ms. Rose a hug. "You did a great job with him."

That night, I modeled my ensemble to my bridesmaids. I had a lot of bridesmaids; my wedding party was ridiculous, but again it made my mama happy.

She wanted all my brothers in the wedding party because, according to her, "God knows when I'll ever see them in a wedding again as they're all shamefully confirmed bachelors."

That meant that Armand had his Krewe and my brothers as groomsmen. Marc was his best man, having lost in the latest *Call of Duty* game to the rest of the Krewe. On my side, I needed six people. I wasn't that social. I mean, I had some built-in friends like Gelly, my cousin and best friend. She was my matron of honor. Her sister-in-law Shell was also a bridesmaid and, of course, Kayleigh, because we were tight. After that, I relied mostly on family and friends of family and friends. I also had Aurelie, Shell's best friend, Tash, Shell's sister, and one of Gelly's good friends, Sarah.

Just because I didn't know my bridesmaids well, didn't mean we couldn't have a fun bachelorette party. I really loved the spa day that Shell threw for her wedding, so, we booked *La Coupe* for a spa day. After that, we would head to Tante Em's dress shop, *Au Bal*, to try on some dresses and get ready to go out. I had thought about Cowboys Bar, because that was really where I started to get to know Armand, but I decided on the tamer, Little Big Cup, because I wanted food, not liquor.

We got to Little Big Cup and asked for a table on the terrace. We settled at the coziest table next to the Bayou Teche.

"Are y'all ready to order?" My friend, Di, popped up next to the table with water and menus,

"Di! How is your nephew Mack doing?"

"He was offered a free ride at all the big schools."

"Oh, no! He's moving out of state?"

"Nope. I convinced him that Tulane was where he wanted to go. That way he can stay for free with family."

"Yay!" I reached in my purse and pulled out one of the extra invitations, in case I forgot to invite someone. "You're coming to my wedding — well, our convalidation ceremony — but for me, it's my wedding."

Di snickered. "Yes, I remember you learning about your marriage. It was memorable."

"Yes, but this time I get to say, 'I do,'" I said with a smile.

"An important element for a good marriage," she joked. "I'll be back in a few for your orders and I will see you at your wedding." She winked and snatched up the invitation.

Armand

Father LeBrun was out to get me. Ms. Denise and Mr. Herman insisted on the blessing of a church ceremony. Renee, while she pretended not to care, was walking on clouds. So, I bit the bullet. I went to the convalidation counseling sessions, where I was read the riot act about marrying by proxy. Also, I knew it was a requirement, but I felt Father LeBrun took particular glee in telling me we needed to abstain from 'congress,' as he called it.

"But we just got back in the same room!" I whined to Renee as we left Father LeBrun's office.

"Whose fault is that? Also, it's only for a little while."

Thank goodness I had a room right next to her. We would make out and snuggle and talk. It wasn't as terrible as I thought it would be, but parting at night was painful.

Days of planning dragged on. Finally, it was our wedding day. I woke up in my little cave and went to wake up Renee with a kiss, but she had already left. My suit for the day was laid out on the bed, along with a letter with my name in cursive on the envelope.

> *Cher Armand,*
>
> *Today is the wedding we deserved. Thank you for taking care of us when you thought you wouldn't be back. I know your heart was in the right place. Now, our hearts are together. That doesn't mean I'll never get mad again and throw things at you. I'm sure I will, but I'll aim to miss. Unless you really piss me off. With that said, I want to underline <u>that I love you, all of you.</u> I love your strengths and your weaknesses. I will meet you at church. I'll be the one in the big floofy dress.*
>
> *Je t'aime — and I always will,*
>
> *Renee*
>
> *P.S. My parents have the twins. We will all meet up after the ceremony.*

Smiling, I folded her letter and put it in the inside pocket of the suit jacket that Renee had laid out on the bed. Then I smelled the bacon. My mama had started fixin' breakfast for me and the Krewe. Renee's brothers had already arrived and were eating.

"Good morning," I greeted everyone as I walked into the kitchen. Mama handed me a cup of coffee, and I grabbed the notepad off the fridge. "I'll be right back."

I laid down on our bed and thought for a moment.

> *Chère Renny,*
>
> *I'm looking forward to this ceremony. I want to tell the world you're mine. Just to let you know, I have a surprise for you as well. A way for you to occasionally get mad at me without damaging more of your mawmaw's ceramic figurines. Wait and see. Until then, I want you to know that I love you and our babies, and I'll do everything in my power to love, care for, and protect you. I'll meet you at church. I'll be the one in the fancy suit.*
>
> *Je t'aime pour toujours,*
> *Armand*

I folded the note, taped it shut, and then asked Oscar to deliver it for me.

"Not a footman," he insisted.

"Please!" I begged, and he relented, shaking his head like I was crazy. I might just be. Before breakfast, I went around the house, strategically placing my surprises for Renee — Nerf balls in every nook and cranny.

After breakfast, we dressed and headed to the church. Father LeBrun nodded to me and directed me to where I needed to stand. It felt like I was standing there forever. Marc kept nudging me and trying to distract me, but my attention was focused firmly on the door. Then the music started.

It seemed like we had the largest wedding party on the planet. Val, Bailey Marie, and Sofia skipped down the aisle flinging and scattering rose petals at everyone, and then Tanner walked down the aisle with our rings. The rest of my Krewe and Renee's brothers all came in with bridesmaids on their arms. When the music changed, the doors opened, and there she was: my Valkyrie.

"Chin up off the ground," Marc snickered.

Renee grinned when she saw my expression and then we just stared at each other as Mr. Travis walked her down the aisle.

The rest of the ceremony was a blank, except where Father LeBrun told me I could kiss the bride.

"Finally," I said, and I pulled her into my arms, kissing her until Marc nudged me.

We walked down the aisle to claps and Ms. Amelie saying, "It's about time."

Epilogue

Renee

Our reception was held at the Little Big Cup restaurant. Nearly the whole town was there, and I couldn't wait to leave. My mama and daddy would be taking the twins for the night. After weeks of abstinence with Armand kissing me silly and then disappearing into his room, I was out of patience. I think we stayed at our reception for an hour tops. Enough to cut the cake, listen to toasts, and share the required dances.

Once everyone was on the dance floor, I grabbed Armand's arm. "Home, now!" I demanded, and he did not need to be told again. We ran to his car and took off like a bat outta hell. When the Challenger slammed to a halt in our driveway, we both ran out, leaving the doors opened. Armand unlocked the front door, opened it, and then grabbed me up fireman style to carry me to our bedroom.

He threw me on the bed and then dove on top of me. His mouth covered mine as his tongue licked in. My legs wrapped around him to bring him even closer, and my fingers pulled at his dark locks. *Closer!* That word repeated in my mind over and over again until we needed to move apart for a breath.

"Clothes ...off." I was beyond complete sentences, and we had just gotten started. He lifted up into a kneeling position as he whipped his shirt off. Then he jumped over me, landed on his feet, and shimmied off his pants and boxers.

"Me, too!" I told him.

He looked down at me with my gold bustier, arm cuffs and hair combs, and shook his head. "I don't think so." He flipped the skirt of my dress up and ripped off my undies.

"Not fair."

"Yes, that's part of the appeal, Valkyrie. I'm sorry, you basically cosplay my wet dreams at the wedding, and then you expect fairness. I don't think so." With that, his head disappeared under my skirt and when he licked into me, I didn't give a damn about fairness. He nipped and sucked at my clit while putting first one finger, then the next, into me. I steadied myself by holding on to the brass bars on the headboard. He teased me to a peak and then would pull away, blowing softly on my sensitive flesh.

After the third time, I growled, "Don't you dare." Then I pushed his head down.

He chuckled against my clit. His words were a warm breeze. "Whatever you want, my Valkyrie." And then he pushed me up again. This time when his finger entered me, it was too much, and it set off a series of explosions, one after the other. Every muscle in my body tensed as I saw first fireworks and then darkness.

I felt Armand's warmth leave me, as he backed away. "My ears may never be the same. Worth it."

My eyes fluttered open, and he was on his knees, staring at me. "Sorry?" A smile spread across my face.

He shook his head. "You don't look very contrite."

I used my leg to hook him and bring him closer. "Not contrite at all."

He leaned over me, a hand on either side of my head and bent his elbows so when he spoke, his lips brushed against mine. "What do you want, Renny?"

"More."

"Your wish." And he spread my thighs and settled against me. His shaft was warm and hard at the entrance of my core. Then he nipped my bottom lip, and his tongue plunged into my mouth, filling it as he slowly pushed inside me. He attempted to pull out, but I locked my legs around him and pushed him back in.

He looked at me. "You think you're in charge?"

I nodded as I gripped with my legs and pushed against him as I swiveled my hips. He groaned. I did it again and again. Each time pulling another groan out of him.

He lifted to look at me. "You ... need ... to ... stop ... that."

I did it again, smirking at him. Then one more time, and he was over the edge. He fell against me and started pounding into me. I would have gloated, but the friction was too much. He gave a final groan, and I came, arching off the bed, scratching his back, my thighs gripping him. Breathing heavily against my neck, he laid there. I was wonderfully crushed beneath him. I couldn't hide my grin. He saw it when he rolled off me.

"Pretty pleased with yourself, Mrs. Leger?"

My eyes met his. I giggled, kissed him softly, and then whispered in his ear, "More."

If you want to stick with the HEA, stay here. If you want to find out more about Kayleigh's story, read on.

Au Suivant

Kayleigh

It was like I was watching from above. I took out the seats of my Subaru and put them in my storage unit. I replaced them with a cot, a sleeping bag, a camp stove, and a cooler. The clothes that I needed were hanging from the hooks where the back seat had been. I had no choice. My money went to cover the costs for Claire's treatment. There was no money left, and even if there had been, Nonc Bill clearly had told my landlord to kick me out.

Luckily, parking wasn't an issue. Everyone at the library was used to seeing my car there when they left at night and when they arrived in the morning. Each paycheck, I spent a little to make car life easier. A twenty-four-hour health club membership meant I had access to a shower and a bathroom. Blackout panels made sure that no one could see I was in my car. To deal with the temperature issues, I purchased window deflectors so I could crack my windows without rain getting in and a fan. Once I started cracking the windows, I needed a magnetic screen to keep the bugs out. It was never ending.

For comfort and safety, I got a below-zero sleeping bag, in case of a cold front. While I also purchased a very expensive memory foam pillow, it did nothing to help me sleep. I walked around each day like a zombie. Food was also an issue. While I had a camp stove, I couldn't use it in the library parking lot. I ended up eating canned or processed foods, or just not eating at all. It was not a sustainable lifestyle, but somehow, I had kept it a secret from my colleagues, friends, and family for months — until I was walking to my car, and I saw creepy Stan with his arms crossed over his chest blocking my driver's side door.

"So, homeless is better than being married to me?" he snarled.

"So much better!" And then he hit me. I woke up in the room I was given. My breath coming in gasps. *Take the good with the bad, Kayleigh.* I may still be homeless. I may be relying on the kindness of others, but, hey, at least now I had running water. At that, I smiled and headed off to take a hot bath.

Read the rest of Kayleigh's story in the holiday romance novel *Noël in Love*. Scan the QR code on the following page.

Also by Gigi Hodge

Louisiana L'Amour Series

Learning to Love: Book 1
Dance of Love: Book 2
Thrown into Love: Book 3
Noël in Love: Book 4
Storm of Love (Novella)
Louisiana L'Amour Omnibus

Louisiana Small Town Romance

The Magic of Chemistry

The Babineaux Brothers

Bayou Catfish

About the Author

Growing up in French Louisiana, Gigi was always a reader. But writing also played a role in her life once she began teaching. She worked with the National Writing project as a teacher and then helped to run a program as a professor. She participated in several Nanowrimo experiences (write a novel in a month) throughout the years. However, after she retired in November 2022, she finally listened to her inner voice and challenged herself to become a published writer.

Important to note: Since Gigi now lives abroad, she often uses her writing to connect to her home and experiences in Louisiana. Most of the restaurants and food in her work are not fictional places, although some of them have closed. Go eat there ... you will appreciate the Louisiana cuisine. Coming from a French Louisiana background, Gigi also includes the occasional French word or expression. She plans to create a Louisiana French bookmark to highlight her most used Cajun/Creole vocabulary.

Acknowledgements

No author is an island. It takes a team to pull together a book. I want to thank mine. So, thanks to my beta readers, Rebecca Klug and Nicole Boudreaux whose insights have been invaluable. I want to thank Holly Schullo for giving me a free line edit, best author gift ever. I also want to thank the All Write Well team for their support and instruction to help me learn how to move from being a hobby writer into a published author.